He thought excitedly of his visions of the gold and the skull in its strange amber glow, of the way the rune had almost pained him, so alive it had been, lying against his chest. "Father, you know what I think? I think that these lines are letters and numbers. And if they are—was Mother—?" He faltered at the shocked expression on Stig's face, then pressed doggedly on. "Was—*is* she a wizard, do you think?"

Stig went a deep red, then to Gom's surprise, he laughed outright. "To tell you the truth, son, she might very well be. 'Twere strange, the way she popped up out of the blue, and disappeared again. And I allus said she wouldn't have left us without good reason. And wizards have good reason. For they have such important work about the world, you know. Why, they really do speak with queens, too. To think," he said, looking wistful, "that she bided full thirteen year with me."

Gom leaned forward, forgetting his broth, his toast, everything. His mother—a *wizard*. How wonderful if it were true!

GRACE CHETWIN has written several books for young readers, including those featuring the boy-wizard Gom Gobblechuck: *The Riddle and the Rune*, *The Crystal Stair*, and *The Starstone*, all available in Laurel-Leaf editions. She lives in Glen Cove, New York.

From *Tales of Gom* in the

LEGENDS OF ULM

BOOK I

— GOM —

ON WINDY

MOUNTAIN

BY

GRACE CHETWIN

Published by
Dell Publishing
a division of
Bantam Doubleday Dell Publishing Group, Inc.
666 Fifth Avenue
New York, New York 10103

ISBN: 0-440-20543-3

RL: 5.2

Reprinted by arrangement with William Morrow & Company, Inc.

Printed in the United States of America

February 1990

10 9 8 7 6 5 4 3 2 1

OPM

For M.C.S.J.
with love.

RUGK

HIGH VARGUE

Quend

Green Vale

agget-on-the-Edge

LONG VALLEY

Lake Langoth

Pen'langoth

SHORE

"You've a singular mind, Gom; knowing and sharp. But at heart you're still a mountain boy and no match for the world out there."

—Stig of Windy Mountain

I

CHAPTER ONE

IGH ON WINDY MOUNTAIN, above the town of Clack, there once lived a woodcutter named Stig. He was a simple man; big, with a big red face, a head shaped like an onion, and a thatch of yellow hair.

Now although he was a good man, a strong man, a proper man, he had no wife. As a matter of fact, the thought of getting himself wed didn't appeal to him at all. If he ever felt lonely, as he might sometimes on a winter's evening, maybe, when the wind blew the snow about his tiny hut, that feeling didn't last *so* long. He was on the whole too busy and happy earning his daily bread on the mountain to think much of anything else. Besides, there was plenty of company up there, of sorts.

One bright spring morning, he took his axe to the place where he was chopping logs to take down into the town. All through the spring and summer and fall, the townsfolk gradually piled his wood higher and higher around the walls of their houses ready for the next winter snows. And in return for the wood, they supplied him with victuals.

He worked and worked at his chopping until the sun shone down through the tops of the trees. Then he stopped and sat up against a stout tree trunk to eat his elevenses: a bit of rough oatcake that he'd made himself on his gray stone hearth, and a swallow of water from an old green glass bottle. While he ate, he looked about him at the wild creatures that came hopping and creeping up for crumbs, close enough for him to touch: sparrows, rock doves, squirrels—even woodchucks—all talking at him a fair lick, and he listened to their chatter, as he did every day, wishing he could understand what it was all about.

That day, a small brown sparrow with quick black eyes hopped with great daring closer than the rest, scolding them and chasing them away, as if wanting to keep Stig to itself. Or rather, *herself*, Stig saw, for the sparrow did not wear the male's neat black bib. Stig scattered a few pieces of the oatcake before her, watched her take them into her beak and break them up, showering surplus crumbs right and left for the rest to scramble for. When she edged forward a mite nearer, her head to one side, Stig laughed delightedly.

"Are you asking for more? If so, here it is." He crumbled more of the oat flakes and scattered them a little closer in than before. The sparrow hopped nearer, and nearer, eyeing him keenly, then dipping down and snatching up a beakful, she flew this time up into the trees to eat it out of range. The other birds, catching the flirt of her wings, all started up after her, and the squirrels followed after, leaving the glade bare.

Stig was not offended. He knew his friends had to be careful and trust no one. Rather he admired their wisdom.

He stood up, threw down the last of the crumbs. "If only I were as careful in my affairs," he called to them, "I'd be a richer man."

But he wasn't really serious. If the folk down in Clack took a little advantage of him, and cheated him in their weekly bartering, he didn't take it ill. He had enough food to eat, and wood for warmth. And if his clothes were a bit threadbare, what mattered that on the mountain with no one to see him?

Not that their cheating amounted to much. On the whole, the townsfolk were kind to him. He'd gotten many a hand-me-down suit from friendly wives who'd sewn their husbands new ones. One wife had even given him an old patchwork quilt. (Patchwork quilts made from scraps of worn-out clothing were a specialty of the thrifty towns-women.)

Along with these kind gifts he'd also gotten a deal of advice that sometimes bordered on nagging. You should get married, the wives told him, just about every time he went down into the town. Have someone to keep you company; to cook for you and wash for you and keep your house clean. But for all the nagging, Stig knew he was safe enough, so safe he was even bold enough to challenge them.

"Who will wed me, then? Come on. Find me a maid to go back up the mountain with me, to live as a wood-cutter's wife!" Of course, they were unable to think of a soul who would leave the comfort and company of the town to share Stig's bare little hut up on the lonely mountain-side.

And so, Stig would escape back home whistling and singing, so relieved and happy to be alone that he'd even made up a song about it, which he sang every day on the way home from his work.

> High on Windy Mountain,
> Stig lives a simple life;
> He has but a bed,
> A roof over his head,
> And a hearth unencumbered by wife.

Whatever Stig felt, he told it in song, all the day long; whether he was alone in his hut, or out on the mountainside. Every fine day his rich warm voice would carry over the wind, and down in Clack they could hear him coming for miles.

And in the winter, when the snows came, smothering the mountain and shutting Stig indoors, he'd sit by his hearth, still singing away, making simple wooden carvings of his wild friends to trade down below. As he finished them, he'd place them against the walls of the hut until those walls were fairly crowded with squirrels, woodchucks, sparrows, blue jays, rabbits; and his night friends, raccoons and owls. And what wonderful carvings they were, especially the figures of the owls. There were screech owls, cat owls, marsh owls, and Stig's own favorite, his friend the old hoot owl who lived in the hollow tree across the clearing from his front door. These he loved to make from good knotty branches, using the knobbles for the head and the knots for the great, round eyes, into the center of which, when they were finished and polished, he set tiny black seeds that shone in the firelight.

Right now, however, it was late spring, a very mild and friendly late spring at that, and he had a heavy day's work to do chopping up an old oak felled by the last winter's storms.

He worked and worked away until the sun was down over the tops of the trees, and his body was crusted with the salt of his sweat. His belly began to rumble pleasantly.

He began to think of a cold dip in the creek on his way home, of lighting the fire ready laid in his hearth to boil water for his tea, of the bread and cheese he'd eat for his supper while sitting on his doorstep—a real treat after being shut up in his hut over the long winter months. The cheese was a bit sweaty by now, even though he kept it in the root cellar, and the bread was a mite stale, but he didn't mind, for it was all that he was used to, living up there alone without the time to cook the fancy suppers that the townsfolk enjoyed every night.

His friend the hoot owl was just waking up and the first star was out as he climbed the last slope to his hut, singing as ever, his favorite song:

> High on Windy Mountain,
> Stig lives a simple life;
> He has but a bed,
> A roof over his head,
> And a hearth . . .

He stopped.

His hut door was open, and from it across the mild spring air were coming the most delicious smells of roasting meats and baking breads and herbs.

He walked the last steps, pushed back the door, and went inside.

CHAPTER TWO

HE HEARTH WAS CLEANLY swept—more cleanly than Stig had ever managed. Over it bubbled Stig's old big black pot—so scoured and scrubbed it looked like new—and from the pot came the smell of herbs. Before the hearth was stacked a pile of creamy-brown muffins, higher, much puffier than Maister Lardle's—(the baker down in Clack). Beside it was a large brown loaf of bread, all crusty and flaky, just how Stig liked it. At the other end of the hearth was a big blue covered plate. And from the plate came the smell of roast meat and potato.

The floor had been scrubbed until the tiny stars in the gray flagstones gleamed in the light of the fire, and the brown wooden walls were clear of cobwebs. The one small window opposite the hearth had been polished until it shone in the glow of the flames, while by the far wall, facing the door, the bed, Stig's narrow cot, was covered with a bright blanket made from crocheted shapes of suns and moons and stars, all joined together with a curious vinelike lattice stitch worked in black yarn. The shabby old quilt that the townswoman had given him was neatly folded on the floor beside it.

All this Stig smelt and saw, but the seeing he did with only half an eye. For in the center of the new-scrubbed floor, on the only (upright) chair, sat the strangest person he had ever seen. She was dressed all in brown, from her brown shirt and shawl to her long brown skirt and boots buttoned down the sides. Her dark brown hair was pulled back tightly over her ears into a bun at the nape of her neck. Around her neck was a leather thong and on the thong hung a strange device that looked like this:

Beside her was a brown canvas bag stuffed full of—what? Stig couldn't clearly see, but tied to the handle were a kettle, a small saucepan, and a water bottle made of hide.

He stood there for quite a minute staring at the person sitting in the middle of his hut with her hands crossed quietly in her lap, her eyes fixed on him without so much as a blink. In fact, he might have gone on staring for a while longer had she not spoken first.

"Good evening, Stig," she said. Her voice was low and a little hoarse, as though she had a sore throat.

Stig kept on staring. How old was she? He couldn't tell. She was certainly no maid, yet she did not look like a crone. She was no beauty, even Stig could tell that. Her skin was not russet-cream and smooth like the townswomen's, but yellow-brown and weathered as the flesh of an old chestnut. She had a long narrow face, a long crooked nose, and eyes quick and black as little buttons. On the end of her chin were three brown moles.

When Stig did not answer her, she stood, reaching but midway up Stig's chest. "Here," she said. "Sit you down. You look tired. And hungry. Do you like broth?" She went to the hearth and stirred the pot, sending a cloud of fragrant steam into the room.

Stig watched her, slowly ruffling up his hair.

"Who are you?" he asked. "And where do you come from?"

She straightened up and turned around. "I come from over the mountains." She held out the broth ladle. Stig took it, and sipped. Delicious. She nodded, bent down, and took up Stig's only two bowls from where they were warming in the hearth, and filled them. She pointed to the chair. "Sit," she said.

Stig, coming to his senses, shook his head. "I like to take my supper at the door."

"Go and sit there, then," she told him. "Make yourself comfortable, and I'll bring it to you."

Stig sat himself down on the stoop, facing out toward the hoot owl's hollow tree, and no sooner was he settled than the strange woman handed him a bowl of broth and a chunk of the new-baked bread. Then she came to the door with a bowl also, and sat cross-legged on the ground beside him, looking out with him over the peaceful glade, and breathing deep of the evening air.

The sun by now was below the trees, and the spaces between them had grown dark and mysterious. In a little while the hoot owl would pop his head out of his hollow tree, hoot a greeting, and fly off as he always did to find his own supper, leaving Stig to get on with his.

Stig stared at the curious pendant hanging from the

woman's neck. It was exquisitely fashioned, carved out of some shiny black stone that he'd never seen before. He wanted to take it up, touch it, examine the cunning blade work, but he'd never dream of doing such a thing. So instead he asked, "What's that?"

The woman put down her spoon and lifting the pendant over her head, handed it to him. "It's my rune," she said.

"Rune?" He turned the small thing over in his great palm, studying it closely. Cut into the hard stone were tiny sharp designs so minute that he could scarce pick them out, especially in the poor light. There were short straight lines, crisscrossed, long curly ones winding in and out, and small bosses tiny as a pinhead surrounded by circles, slashed. The workmanship was so fine that he himself would have been proud to have done such on wood. But on stone? He shook his head in wonder.

"It stands for my name. It is my secret charm." The woman smiled, and in the dusk, with the glow of the firelight behind her it seemed to Stig that she looked almost beautiful.

Stig nodded. Charms he did understand. The townsfolk used them all the time: anything from crossed fingers to sprigs of dried herbs tied with wild onion shoots to keep the butter from turning sour in the churn, to make rain for the crops, to protect babies in the womb. The idea of a secret charm like this one standing for someone's name, however, was new.

"Why, what is your name?" he asked her.

"If I told you that," she said, "my rune would lose its power."

Stig handed back the pendant. "Then what shall I call you?"

She took it, replaced it about her neck, and picked up her broth again. "Nay," she said. "That's for you to decide, presently."

Now what did she mean by that, Stig wondered, and would have asked her, that and many more questions, such as where she was going, and why, and how she was going to travel that night down the dark mountain by herself, but instead, filled with a sudden deep sense of peace, he simply sat back and cleaned up his bowl as though he'd been doing it for years and years. And his plate of meat and potatoes. And muffins, three of them.

"Thank you for sharing your food with me. You certainly cooked it well," he said.

"You're more than welcome," she replied. "It only lightened my load." She handed him one more muffin, which he hadn't the strength to refuse.

By the time he sat back at last, it was dark. Over the tops of the trees the moon rose round and full and tiny gray moths fluttered in the firelight from the open door. In the distance, the hoot owl called.

Stig stirred, got up, and went to get the bucket for water to clean the dishes, but the woman beat him to it, much to his surprise, for he was sure she wouldn't be strong enough to carry the bucket full from the spring, it being heavy enough even when empty.

So he sat again and sang softly, first to himself, then for both of them while she rattled the dishes around in Stig's wooden washtub that he kept on top of the root cellar lid at the side of the hut. As she washed, Stig watched her hands, with their fingers, quick and deft. Work hands. And strong. But small and very fine.

The woman asked him to sing more, and he did, though he was not sure afterward what about, but he had a hazy recollection that she'd wanted to hear about the mountain and the town below. He sang songs for chopping wood, songs for waking up the morning and going off to work; songs of his wild friends, songs of his larger friends down in the town below; of crop sowing, wash days, and harvest festivals—even rowdy ale songs that the young lads had taught him on the rare occasions when he'd stayed down there overnight. And while he sang, she came back to sit on the step, let out her long thick hair, and brushed it with a stiff wire brush, braiding it into a pigtail down her back. Such thick hair. Beautiful.

Stig sang on, thinking what comfortable company she was, sitting there listening to so many of his favorite songs, one after another, and laughing with him sometimes at the words. When he was done, he was rarely tired.

"Up," Stig heard the woman say from a long way off. He opened his eyes, found himself leaning with his back against the door lintel, his head drooping on his chest. He stood up and went inside. The fire was low, the ashes raked out. The cover of the little bed was neatly turned down.

He scratched his head, looking around.

"It's dark," he said. "The paths down the mountain are traitorous to those who don't know them. You'll likely come to grave harm out there."

"Then I'd best stay here," she said, "if you don't mind."

Stig glanced worriedly at his bed, which looked so bright and soft and attractive in the embers of the fire. He certainly didn't mind giving her shelter for the night, especially after she had cooked him such a treat of a supper. But where would she sleep? He went over to the bed, lifted a corner of the crocheted blanket. "Is this yours?" he asked the woman.

"It was," she said. "But now it's yours, in return for your hospitality."

Stig's worried face smoothed out. He pulled the blanket from the bed and threw it about his shoulders. "In that case," he said, "since you're my guest, please make yourself comfortable. It's warm tonight out in the clearing. I'll sleep there. I shall lie on my quilt, and cover myself with your blanket. Goodnight."

He went out, shutting the door behind him. Then, spreading the quilt under the hoot owl's hollow tree, he lay down and pulled the crocheted blanket over him and slept as soundly as ever he had in all his life.

* * *

The next day, he awoke to the smell of hot toasting pancakes.

He opened his eyes, staring up into misty branches, wondering for a moment where he was. Then he was on his feet and through the door to find the woman already up and dressed with the bed made and the fire burning brightly. Over the flames the woman was making a stack of golden corn cakes in her little frying pan.

She pointed to a pile on the hearthstone.

"Eat," she said. "There are plenty more."

Stig squatted beside the hearth while she handed him a plate piled with a dozen pancakes drenched in honey. She must have been carrying that with her, Stig decided, for he hadn't any. In fact, he hadn't tasted any for months for it was not often that he could afford it. He ate one pancake, then two, and three, and four, and kept going until they were all gone. He helped them down with a mug of strong black tea with a generous helping of honey in it, dunking a muffin left over from the night before.

After that, it was time for him to go to work.

He stood up, went to wash his plate.

"Leave that," she said. "You just go about your work. Go on," she prompted him when he lingered. "And don't worry about the fire. I'll take care of that, too."

He went outside, took up his axe, and stood awkwardly looking toward the open door. "Goodbye," he called. "And a good journey to you."

The woman called him back, holding out his knapsack. In it was bread, some meat and potato from last night's supper, and water in the old green glass bottle. He'd been so bewuthered at her being there that he'd clean forgotten his elevenses. But she hadn't. He took the knapsack, shouldered his axe, and strode away across the clearing.

He worked hard all that day, thinking about the night before, about what good company the woman had been, about how much he had enjoyed singing for her. He wondered a little sadly where she was by then. Through the town and out probably, and gone for good, for folk seldom came to Clack, and never twice.

He stopped as usual when the sun struck down through the trees, and leaning his back against the tree trunk, threw remnants of the woman's crusty bread to his wild friends, which cheered him up no end. So much so that he sang, loud and strong, happy songs of his work on the mountain, and the joy of his simple life. But when the sun began to go down over the treetops and it was time for him to bathe in the creek, his songs became quieter.

He dove into the creek and swam underwater, as usual, to the other side, then back again. But he didn't splash, or snort, or slap the water with the palm of his hand for joy as he usually did. He just scrubbed himself down and got dressed in silence, not having the heart to sing anything, somehow.

And when at last it was time for the last lap home and

his freedom song, he almost didn't give voice to that.

Bravely, however, he began his song, as he strode the last slope toward the clearing in front of his dark and empty hut.

> High on Windy Mountain,
> Stig lives a simple life;
> He has but a bed,
> A roof over his head,
> And a hearth . . .

He stopped as an unmistakable and delicious mixture of smells hit his nose. He half strode, half ran the last few steps, broke through the trees to find the hut door open and firelight flickering on the walls inside.

As he crossed the clearing, the woman appeared in the doorway and beckoned. "Quick," she said. "Sit you down and make yourself comfortable. It's root pie and carrot cake today and they're ready for the eating. You came just right."

* * *

"But," he said, finishing off the last of the carrot cake. "You didn't go. And now it's all dark again, and as I told you, the trail's not safe for one who doesn't know its ways."

"Then," she said, pushing past him to fill the bucket for the dishes, "I'd best stay again. But this time, I'll sleep outside."

CHAPTER THREE

OR THREE NIGHTS MORE Stig returned home to find the woman still there and delicious smells of cooking and baking drifting out from his door over the mountainside.

And each night Stig went a mite faster, and earlier, hoping more and more that he would find her still there, fearing that she might be gone. Every night one of them took a turn sleeping out in the clearing, Stig never mentioning now the trail leading down into the town in case she was minded to take it, she never referring to it either, to his great relief.

On the fourth night, as Stig walked homeward, he looked up through the trees. All day the air had been heavy, and sooty clouds were now piling up overhead. There was going to be a storm.

It broke halfway through supper.

There was a big clap of thunder, a quick flash of lightning, and the rain began to spatter down. They dodged back into the hut and shut the door behind them.

The woman made him sit in the chair, while she squatted by the hearth.

"You've been working hard all day," she said. "You'd best rest your bones now."

"But you're the guest," he said. "It doesn't seem right for you to sit like that on the floor. I see I'll have to make another chair." When he realized what he'd said he stopped, feeling his ears burning, but the woman seemed not to have noticed.

He sat awkwardly, staring into the fire, eating the last of his supper, slowly thinking over what he'd just said. It occurred to him then that neither of them would be sleeping outside that night. Oh well, he thought, he'd be just as comfortable lying by the fire.

The woman took Stig's plate and set it with hers and the rest of the dishes by the door. They'd have to wait until morning, she said. And with that she went back to her place by the hearth.

Just then a gust of wind rattled the walls around them and pulled at the roof, so that for a minute Stig feared the hut would be snatched from over their heads, and he couldn't help but think then how nice it was to have someone to be cozy with on that wild night.

"It looks like the rain's setting in," Stig said. He shifted awkwardly in his chair, wanting to get up and give her his seat, but not wanting to offend her either. "I hope as it's over by tomorrow night, for I go down into the town the day after tomorrow, and the trail's fair terrible after a big rain. The cart slips and slides and it's all I can do to get it down, even with straps and ropes and all."

"The day after tomorrow?" The woman looked at him thoughtfully, and Stig felt a stab of worry. Was she thinking of going down the trail with him? Down to the town and on her way at last?

He was just wondering this when suddenly the wind blew down through the chimney, filling the little hut with thick black smoke that set them coughing and crying and running to the door.

It fairly burst open in Stig's hands. The rain lashed in, drenching them, flooding the floor, and the wind blew up the chimney now as well as down, sending ash and soot and more smoke all over the place.

Together, they slammed the door, jammed the chair against it, then ran about clearing up the mess as best they could. By the time they'd done, Stig saw that the woman's neat brown hair was feathered in ash and her face was fairly piebald. He raised a hand to his mouth to stifle a laugh, saw the soot on it, and realized that he must look no better. His laugh escaped his fingers. Seeing at once the cause of it, the woman joined in, and together they laughed loud and long.

"Oh dear," the woman said, wiping her eyes on her shawl, streaking her face with soot and tears. "That was good. It's been a while since I laughed like that."

"Likewise here," said Stig. He waved the woman to his chair. "Your turn, ma'am," he said. "I insist."

The woman shrugged, sat, and folded her hands in her lap while Stig settled himself down by the hearth, with his back against the mantel, just as though it were a tree trunk.

"This," Stig said, nodding his head toward the window, "is as bad as I've seen it rain up here."

The woman nodded. "I've seen worse. Why, last year

coming through the Skilly Hills, I saw a whole town washed clean away. Houses floating along with the flood like great boats, the folks sitting on the rooftops waving their hats to you as they passed, and cows and goats tied to the chimneys—and hens perched atop of *them*!"

Stig leaned forward. Neither he nor any of the townsfolk had been out of the mountain valley. "The Skilly Hills? Where are they? Are they far from here?"

The woman told him about the Skilly Hills, and about lots of other wonders, and by the time she had done Stig was slumped against the mantel, his eyes half closed.

Just outside the window, a cardinal whistled.

Stig jumped up. "Good heavens!" he cried. "It's morning." He went to the door, opened it. The rain had stopped. And the wind. The air was fresh and clear and cool. The sky above was turning that pale shade of green you get sometimes at sunrise after lots of rain.

What a wonderful storyteller the woman was, to be sure. Why he'd passed the whole night away without knowing it, and he didn't feel in the least bit tired.

The woman came up behind him, picked up the dishes by the door. "Come," she said. "I'll wash these and get you some breakfast together. It's almost time for you to go to work."

He stayed in the doorway, blocking it. "Nay," he said. "I'll not go to work today. I've a mind to go down into town."

"Oh? And whyfor?" The woman fixed her eyes on him keenly. "You said tomorrow was your town day."

He shuffled his feet and looked at the floor. "I know I did, but now I have business that can't wait," he said. "So I'm taking the wood down today, and you too, if you'll agree."

"Oh? Whyfor?"

"It's like this." Stig finally managed to look into her face. "You told me to find my own name for you. Well, now I have, and it's 'Wife.'"

CHAPTER FOUR

HEY SET OFF DOWN the trail, Stig pulling on the shafts of the great wood cart as it rolled along before him, ever eager to be out of his grasp and rolling helter-skelter down the steep mountainside. The woman stepped lively alongside, carrying ropes and straps that Stig was surely going to need before long. The steep winding trail was slippery from the rains, and slidey from the loose shale left behind by the overnight flooding.

"I think," said Stig, as the woman dodged a deep puddle, "that it's going to get worse afore it gets better." Sure enough, they reached a spot where the path had given way altogether, leaving a precipice the height of two men. How did they get down? First Stig emptied the cart, then he lowered it hand over hand with a knotted rope (the knots to keep the rope from sliding and burning his hands), until it was firmly wedged on solid, at least *fairly* solid, ground again. After that, he had to get the logs down, then load up once more. All this took some time.

"Why not just throw the wood down?" the Wife suggested.

"Eh, no," Stig replied mildly. "First thing you must learn up on a mountain is never, never to throw anything down anywheres, for there's no knowing where it'll end up, or how much it'll take with it afore it's done. No, these logs must be slid down, one by one, and stacked up below for reloading. And careful, like, so's they don't take off and reach Clack afore us, through someone's roof!"

Despite all he could say, the woman tied up her skirts, rolled up her sleeves, and worked with him, sliding the logs down and stacking them, then hefting them back into the cart.

"Long as this has took," Stig said when they were ready to move on, "it's been nowhere as bad as if I'd had to manage by myself. I thank you heartily for all your trouble." He looked at the woman's muddy boots and torn stockings. "The way is easier from now on," he said. "You'd best climb up onto the cart for the rest of the way—Wife—or you'll have no boots left at all."

He helped her up onto the pile of logs, and settled her comfortably. Then he picked up the shafts and once again set off, maneuvering the bouncing, swaying cart around and around and down into Clack.

What with all the fuss of getting the cart down the trail, it was late when Stig arrived. Breakfast smoke had long risen above thatched roofs from neat whitewashed chimneys as Stig stepped off the trail and onto Clack's main street—its only street, really, that twisted worse than a dog's hind leg, in and out of the shops and houses and the alehouse, The Wild Green Man. The rest of the thoroughfares were but dirt alleyways winding through the backs of the fifty or so haphazard cottages that were the town.

The cart bounced over rough stone cobbles, hard enough to grind a body's bones, so much so that the Wife jumped down again and walked beside Stig, dodging puddles underfoot, and looking about with those quick dark eyes of hers.

The first shop on the main street belonged to Bok, the butcher. Here Stig would always trade wood for bones and dripping and, occasionally, a chop or two. Today he strode past it, the Wife trotting along beside him.

"Hey!" Bok called from his shop doorway. "Stig! What are you doing down here today? And where are you going in such a hurry?"

"Can't stop. I've urgent business," Stig said over his shoulder.

"Urgent business? What sort of business?" Bok shouted after him, but Stig had already gone by.

The butcher stepped out of his shop, closed the door behind him, and followed Stig and the Wife along the street.

Next door, Stig passed the greengrocer's shop.

"Hey!" called Maister Craw, the greengrocer. "What goes on? Aren't you a day ahead of yourself, Stig?"

"I am indeed, Maister Craw. For I have urgent business to attend to."

"Business?"

"That's what he says," Bok said, following behind Stig. "Come on, Maister Craw, let's see what it is."

Maister Craw stepped out of his shop, and closing the door behind him, walked after Stig and the Wife alongside Bok.

Stig walked half the length of the main street that way, past Maister Lardle's bakery, past Maister Corry, the weaver

and sometime tailor. Past the tall twin chimneys of Crick
& Son, potters; and Snag's tannery. Past the smithy, and
Wendle, the shoemaker's shop—("footwear made to last")—
and on until he reached a great bell standing in the middle
of the cobbled way. By this time, he had quite a following
of townsfolk, all curious about the Wife, all obviously
wondering among themselves who she was and what it was
all about, although, as Stig saw, they didn't exactly stare
at her openly.

He set down the cart shafts and mounted the steps up
to the bell. This was the town bell, that tolled for wed-
dings, funerals, and tornadoes. Stig seized the rope and
pulled it good and hard. Not that he'd needed to, for by now
everybody who was anybody was out there to see what was
going on. So when Stig turned away from tolling the bell,
he saw that the townsfolk were already gathered around
him, waiting for him to speak.

He cleared his throat. "I'm getting wed today," he said.
"And this is Wife." He reached for the woman's hand and
drew her forward from around the cart to stand before the
townsfolk.

There was total silence.

"Good for you, Stig!" somebody shouted at last from
the back of the crowd, a young lad's voice by the sound of
it, and there was at once a burst of laughter from that direction. It was immediately stifled, but that cry had pricked
the bubble of silence.

"What's her name?" Bok asked.

"And where's she from?" a huge man called. Pinkle,
the blacksmith, who'd left his anvil to follow the crowd.

"She comes from over the mountains," Stig answered.
"And her name is—" he eyed the woman's rune hanging
from her neck "—Wife."

"Wife? *Wife?* What sort of name is that!" somebody shouted.

" 'Tis a good name. I gave it her myself," Stig said mildly. "A *very* good name, for a good woman. She can cook better than any I know, and sew, and wash and clean, and she is powerful fine company."

There was another awkward silence, until one of the townswomen stepped up, holding out her hand. "Then Wife had best come along," she said. She waved at the brown clothes. "She can't get married in those. She needs something pretty to wear. And flowers. And maids to walk her back to this bell."

Something pretty? Stig looked down at the Wife and ruffled up his hair. "She looks just fine the way she is," he said.

But the Wife moved forward. "That would be nice," she said, smiling, and at once the crowd parted to let her through. A second woman joined her, then a third, until half a dozen of them had gone off with her up the street and out of sight.

At that, the crowd began to buzz. All the men clapped Stig on the back and wished him luck, while Maister Winker, the host of The Wild Green Man, rushed off to break open extra kegs of ale to celebrate with afterward.

Half an hour later, Wife reappeared dressed in a pale blue gown two sizes too big for her, not that Stig noticed particularly, so taken was he with her hair, which the wives had brushed out and braided around her head, and crowned with a garland of forget-me-nots. She still had on her brown boots, though, for only the children had feet as small as hers, but the mud was all cleaned off, and they'd given her new hose to wear.

Stig, too, had on a fancy white shirt that Pinkle's wife

had found for him, and black velvet trousers, which, she said, he could keep (and which Stig happily accepted, not that he could see much use for them back up on the mountain).

At last, Stig and the Wife stood once more before the bell.

"Who will wed us?" Stig asked the crowd.

"I will!" cried Bok, and stepping up beside them, he took of each a hand. He turned to Stig.

"Is this the woman you would wed, Stig, woodcutter of Windy Mountain?"

"Indeed, it is," said Stig.

Bok turned to the Wife. "And is this the man you would wed, Wife, traveler from over the mountains?"

"Aye," said Wife.

"So be it then," said Bok, and with that, he joined their two hands and stepped away. Immediately there was a big cheer and the townsfolk began to dance around them until Stig's head spun.

Pinkle put up his hands and bellowed. "All this cheering and prancing is rare thirsty work! We need ale!"

The crowd parted to let Stig lead the Wife along the street to the alehouse, then surged after them, talking and laughing as though it were a proper festival day.

For hours they sat or stood around, drinking ale, while Stig sang them a song or two. Now and then they all danced to the tune of Maister Sproggins's wheezy bagpipes, and Wife at Stig's instigation even told the tale of the Skilly Hills, which everybody seemed to enjoy, they having just come through the storm and all. And so the time went until Stig, looking up at the sun said, "If we're to get through our business and be back up the mountain before dark, I'd best get to work. So I thank you one and all for me and the

Wife. And," he added, looking around at the townswomen, "let no one say now that I didn't take certain folks's good advice!"

Amid more laughter and cheering, Stig and the Wife went off to change back into threadbare suit and brown skirt and shawl.

Toward late afternoon when the town had returned to its normal routine, and all the wood in Stig's cart was exchanged for new weekly supplies, together with a free bag of beef bones from Bok and a small keg of last year's ale from The Wild Green Man, and when Stig and the Wife finally set off back up the mountain trail, Stig remembered his evening song. He took a deep breath, leaned his head back, and sang loud and clear:

> High on Windy Mountain,
> Stig lives a simple life;
> He has but a bed,
> A roof over his head,
> And a hearth warmed and tended by Wife!

"That's a fine song, Stig," Wife said. "I've a mind to sing it, too. Not that my voice is much to crow about, mind."

"Why, that would be nice. Come to think—listen—I'll sing the first line, then you come in with it just as I start the second. That should sound right pretty."

And it did, so pretty that they sang it, around and around without stopping, all the way home!

CHAPTER FIVE

OR ONE YEAR Stig lived happily with the Wife.

And what a wonderful year that was! Stig had never been more contented in his whole life. He couldn't imagine how he'd ever gotten on alone. He made a large comfortable bed, for which Wife crocheted a fine new cover, just like her first one, only bigger. And this time in among the sun and moon and the stars, she worked other shapes: leaves, flowers, fish, birds, and the small animals Stig loved so well. The smaller blanket she folded over the edge of the bed, ready to warm their feet on cold nights.

Stig also made a second chair, a deep comfortable rocking chair for the Wife, which looked so good he made one for himself. He put in another window to let in more light, and a shelf for Wife's cooking pots.

Every day he'd go off to work singing happily, and every night he'd come home to delicious meals, and a clean and shining hut, and wonderful tales of the wide world outside. Sitting propped against the door frame, he listened enthralled, marveling at what the Wife knew. It worried him sometimes, though, to think how far she'd traveled, how much she'd seen. So many wonders. Sometimes when she was in the middle of a tale, he saw something in the gleam of her dark eyes that made him fear. What? Only when he was going off to sleep at night would he admit what the fear was: that it was all too good to last. That one day she'd go back into that strange wide world never to return.

But he dared not mention it, and Wife seemed content enough with life.

Sometimes she went with him to work, and while he was chopping away, she'd wander off into the trees, coming back with all kinds of leaves and berries and twigs. These she dried and ground and stored on the shelf beside her cooking pots in small glass jars she had taken from her big brown bag. They were herbs, she said, for making her cooking better, but once or twice when Stig came down with coughing and the fever, she made drinks with them that cured him overnight.

At the end of that first year, they had a child. A girl. A large amiable girl with a head shaped like an onion, and a fuzz of yellow hair.

"Well, and isn't that wonderful?" Stig exclaimed, putting out his great hand and gently patting the baby's head. "If she doesn't look just like me!"

Wife nodded solemnly. "Indeed she does, Stig. Indeed she does," she said, cradling the baby in the crook of her arm. She did not return Stig's happy smile.

They called her, Hilsa. When they took her down into town to show all the folk they came back up again loaded with gifts: clothes, a wooden baby tub, and a small patchwork quilt. Stig had refused an old cot, though. He'd already made a cradle for Hilsa himself out of finest oak, carved with figures of animals all around it: ducks swimming among tall straight reeds; rabbits, squirrels, otters, chipmunks, snakes, chasing one another in and out of fern and vine; sparrows and cardinals, and blue jays and mockingbirds flying overhead. And the hoot owl that Stig liked so well to carve? He took the perch of honor, above the baby's head, presiding over all.

In no time at all Hilsa was up on her feet and running around and too big for the cradle—which was just as well, for the second baby arrived, a boy, big and amiable with a head shaped like an onion, and a head of yellow fuzz.

"By all that is wonderful!" Stig exclaimed, ruffling up the baby's hair. "If the boy isn't just like me too!"

The Wife, sighing, agreed. "We shall have to bring a goat up from town, Stig," she said. "Growing children need extra milk and butter and cheese for growing bones."

Stig nodded, looking down at the baby. That one was big enough already, and getting bigger by the minute. Stok, they called him, and when they took him down into town to show, they came back up the mountain loaded with gifts for him: a tiny mug and plate; a gourd-rattle, encased in silver lattice if you please, by Pinkle himself; and a small patchwork quilt.

And . . . a goat. A black-and-white nanny goat that they tethered at the edge of the clearing by the cabin door.

Stig made a small bed for Hilsa along the back wall of the hut, and a chest to keep the children's things in.

A year later, another baby was born, and the next, another, all big and amiable and looking just like Stig. Stig was delighted. He made the hut bigger, built more beds along the back wall, and made more chests for the children to keep their things in.

The Wife, looking not as content as Stig thought she

might, did her part no less, tending the children, teaching the older ones the housecrafts; how to cook, and to wash and sew. How to care for themselves and one another, so that when she went into the woods with Stig sometimes to find her special herbs and seeds and berries, or down into the town with him, the children were perfectly able to manage without her.

"Always, children," she would say, "always a body must be able to stand alone, just as the animals out there."

And she would gaze across the clearing with a strange, faraway gleam in her eye that reminded Stig of the early days when she'd spoken of the great world yonder, and the old fear came back that she'd go off again one day and leave him. But she couldn't, surely, he reassured himself. She wouldn't. They'd been together too long.

Besides, there were the children to bind her to him, especially the sixth child, Horvin, born in a thunderstorm and not quite so amiable as the rest, even if he looked it at first glance. That one cried a lot, and no one would comfort him but the Wife. Surely she couldn't leave Horvin, Stig thought, watching her rocking the child to sleep. Or any of the others, so the more the merrier.

But after the birth of the seventh child, Stig began to change his mind about having so many children running underfoot. "Wife," he said, "this must stop. There isn't room enough, or food to go around."

But the Wife only sighed and nodded, saying nothing.

At the birth of the eighth child, large and amiable, with a head shaped like an onion and a fuzz of yellow hair, Stig grew even more anxious. "Wife," he said. "This must be the last child. The hut isn't big enough to hold any more."

But the Wife only sighed and nodded, saying nothing.

Stig raised the roof beam and made a low loft for the older children to sleep in, leaving the latest baby to sleep in the owl cradle, and the next to the latest one to sleep in Hilsa's old cot by the back wall. This way, with more room to move, things went easier for a while.

But a year later, what do you know but a ninth child arrived, looking as ever, just like Stig.

Stig ruffled up his hair. "Wife, Wife. When will this stop?" He looked about him helplessly, then seeing how solemn the Wife was looking, he smiled and wagged his finger at her, pretending to scold her. "If we have one more child, I'll have to pack you off back where you came from!"

But the Wife didn't smile. She only looked down at the yellow head and sighed, saying nothing.

The next year, to Stig's great relief, no child came. Nor the next, nor the next.

The spring of that year passed, and summer, and so came the fall: a time of rich ripe reds and golds and browns. Stig was at his busiest, taking wood down into the town almost every day, to bring back enough cartloads of grain and root for his large family's winter stores. Stok went with him. "My right hand," his father called him, even though the boy did drag his heels at times. "Never mind," Stig told him often enough. "Some's born woodcutters, and some have to work at it. But the second's no worse than the first. . . ."

The days got shorter, and sharper, until, all too soon, there was frost in the air. *All too soon* because the root cellar was nowhere near full enough to last the winter. Still Stig kept going, working hard up and down the mountain trail with wood, until one misty morning in October, Stig awoke to find the Wife's place beside him in the wide bed empty and cold. He raised his head in the early light and looked around. "Wife?" he called softly. There was no reply. Maybe she'd gone up into the children's loft, he decided.

He climbed out of bed to see, and noticed at once a

small bundle lying in the warm hearth. He went over and touched it. It stirred, and waved a tiny fist. Another child! The tenth, and latest one, lying wrapped in that very first blanket crocheted with suns and moons and stars that the Wife had brought with her those many years ago.

And what a child!

Stig lifted the cover aside. Its skin was yellow-brown and wrinkled as the flesh of an old chestnut, and its head was covered in dark brown hair. There it lay, squirming and kicking by the hearth—and looking up at him, Stig would swear, looking straight up at him with already opened eyes that were quick and black as little buttons.

Stig ruffled his hair, staring down at the baby. "Why," he exclaimed to himself, "if it isn't like the Wife!" He bent down and picked it up, and as he did, something fell off the cover.

Stig, frowning, stooped and retrieved it.

Why, it was the Wife's rune on its leather thong. He turned it over and over, wondering what it could be doing lying on top of the newborn baby. The Wife's rune, her charm, that stood for her secret name. Stig looked at it with misgiving. During all the thirteen years he'd known her, she'd never taken it from around her neck, except that once, to show it to him. In sudden alarm, he remembered his threat to her. *If we have but one more child, I shall have to pack you off back where you came from.*

He looked to the shelf. The cooking pots were still there, but the small glass jars were gone. He looked to the corner where she kept her big brown bag. It was not there. With the baby still in his arms, he ran outside, across the clearing and off to the left where the trail led down into Clack.

He raised himself up as high as he could, peering out through the trees. The trail was empty.

"Wife! Wife! Come back!" he called. "I never meant what I said!" His voice sounded across the treetops, and the echoes went far on the high morning air.

There was no answer.

Hilsa, still in her nightshirt, appeared sleepily in the doorway. "What is it, Father?" she asked him. Then, "Where's Mother?"

Stig didn't even hear her. It's all your fault, he scolded himself, still looking down the empty trail. You told her she'd have to leave, and now she's gone and done it! At that moment, the baby screwed up its face and began to yell. It was hungry.

He turned and hurried back to the hut. "Hilsa," he said. "The goat—get some milk, quick!"

As Hilsa went for milk from the goat, Stig shouted again at the top of his voice: "Forget what I said about the child! We'll manage—with just as many more children as you like. Only come back!"

As the echoes died, the baby quit yelling, as though listening.

Stig waited, and listened too, but all he heard was the wind sighing through the high pines and rattling the broom pods below.

At last, sadly, he went inside and closed the door behind him.

CHAPTER SIX

LL THAT DAY Stig sat, his work forgotten, looking out across the clearing, waiting for Wife to come back. But she didn't.

That night, Hilsa made supper—a good supper, for Wife had taught her well how to cook. Hilsa was twelve now, and big, reaching to her father's shoulder. A credit to her mother's training, thought Stig proudly. As all the children were, the older ones looking after the younger ones, just as Wife had taught them to, Hilsa taking special care of the new baby, and everybody helping with something, even the youngest—not counting the brand-new baby, of course.

Their mother was gone off on business, Stig told them, so that they wouldn't fuss. And they didn't, for a while. Wife had gone into the woods before alone and not come back all day.

But the day passed, and night came, and the children began to grow fretful.

"How much longer, Father?" Hilsa asked him, handing him his supper.

"I don't rightly know." Stig took his plate, set it aside. "But the business must be very important. For your mother wouldn't leave us lightly. That I do know."

The children took their meal inside around the table that Stig had built for them, but Stig sat out on the stoop, as he always had, staring out across the clearing. Every now and again, he'd walk slowly across it and stare out to the left, down the trail, then go back to take his seat on the step. Then he even stopped doing that, but just sat, looking down at his boots. When the hoot owl flew by overhead, Stig didn't even notice. And his plate remained untouched.

The children were late getting to sleep. One or two of them had begun to cry for the Wife, especially Horvin, and it was all Stig and Hilsa could do to comfort them. When at last they were quiet, Stig went to sit for a bit by the hearth, rocking himself and looking at Wife's empty chair.

Horvin crept down the ladder from the loft and ran to his knee. Horvin, the sixth child, born in the thunderstorm. While the others took completely after Stig, showing no sign of the Wife in them either inside or out, this child, his father would swear, had a pinch of his mother's salt in him, with a generous dose of pepper common to neither parent.

"It's *it*, isn't it, Father," he cried, jabbing his finger toward the new baby in the cradle beside the hearth. "She's gone because of *it*."

"Hush, now." Stig, holding Horvin tightly to his chest, patted his golden head. "Not *it*," he said absently. "*Him*." Then, realizing, he held Horvin out at arm's length. "Why, whatever makes you say that?"

"I heard. You told Mother—" Horvin began to cry.

Stig pulled him close again. "There, there," he said. "It's not true. It were only a joke, and your mother knowed it. She's gone off on business, just as I said. She'll be back, you see. Say, do you remember the story she told us about the rains that washed a whole town away?" Before the boy could answer, Stig lifted him onto his knees and started to tell the tale of the Skilly Hills, word for word as near in the way of the Wife as he could. Horvin resisted, but at last his eyes closed. Stig carried him up to bed and laid him down on the crowded floor. He stood about him in the darkness of the loft looking around at all the golden heads, from aged twelve down to three, and sighed. Had he driven the Wife away? He'd told Horvin not. And he was surely right. For he was coming to think that she'd gone off for a reason known only to herself. Good as she'd always been, he had to admit that she'd always been close.

But that was as may be. Whatever happens, he told himself stoutly, I'll not hear bad of her. She were a good woman, and a wonderful wife.

Before he lay down to sleep in the great wide bed, he lit a lamp and hung it in the window beside the door. The night after, he did the same, and the next, and the next.

But the Wife didn't come back.

Every night when he came home, things had gotten worse. Much as the Wife had trained the children to be independent, things grew daily more and more out of hand. They began to fight and to sulk about doing their chores, and it was more than Hilsa and Stig could do to get them all washed and ready for bed at night.

"They're missing Mother," Hilsa said.

"And they're not getting enough to eat," Stig said. "Poor children. I can't guess how Wife managed to make the food go around, but somehow it doesn't anymore. And how she managed to cope with the bumps and scrapes and sneezles and the washing and the ironing and the darning and the cleaning, I'll never know." He ruffled Hilsa's hair. "Go to bed. You look tired out."

"Father—" Hilsa put her hand on her father's arm. "Will she never come back?"

"I'm sure she will," Stig said, but truth to tell, he was beginning to wonder. He was also beginning to worry if something bad had happened to her. The comfort he took was in the pendant hanging from the baby's cradle. It were as though she'd tried to tell him something by leaving it, but he couldn't quite see what. But then she'd always been too deep for him.

That night as he went to bed, he worried also about his family. They were becoming too much for him. In no time they'd have outgrown the hut and then what would he do? And what would they be when they grew up? He sighed and pulled the covers up to his chin.

He would have to face that problem soon.

* * *

The day after that, it was time for him to go down into the town.

"You stay home today," he told Stok. "Help your sister," he said. "She's sorely in need of it."

He left Hilsa with the new baby, and a list of chores for the rest to do to keep them out of mischief. At last, he set off for the town.

Down below, they said to him, "Whatever is the matter, Stig? We can usually hear you coming for miles but today you steal down on us like the mountain mist. What has happened to your song?"

Stig leaned sadly on his cart.

"We have another child and—"

"*Another* child?"

"—and Wife's disappeared," he said.

"Disappeared! Heavens! Oh, you poor, poor man!"

"Has she had an accident, do you think? The mountain can be an uncertain place," said Bok.

"I don't know," Stig answered him. "I hope not. I woke up the day the baby arrived to find her gone."

"Will she be back, do you think?" asked someone.

Stig spread his great hands. "I don't know. I really don't know. But I'm coming to fear not, somehow."

"Easy come, easy go," somebody muttered.

Stig stared about him miserably. Kind as they had been to Wife, the townswomen had never really taken to her. A foreigner born, a foreigner she'd stayed, and they'd never asked her down to wives' suppers or stitching bees and such like. Not after the first year or so. I don't gossip, you see, my dear Stig, the Wife had told him. Don't mind them. They don't know any better, and they've been as kind to me as they can possibly be.

For Wife's sake, Stig stood there, pretending he hadn't heard.

Said one townswoman, "Whatever are you going to do?"

Stig ruffled up his hair. "I don't know. The children are growing and growing, and already the hut's too small for them, and there's not enough food to go around. I don't know how the Wife managed these past years."

"Stig," one woman cried. "You just bring those dears down here and we'll take care of them."

"Oh, but I couldn't," Stig said. "I'm their father. They need me. And—what if the Wife came back?"

"Fathers are all very well," another said, "but children

of that age need a mother more. And if the Wife comes back, you could say we were looking after them temporary. And take them up the mountain again."

Maister Craw spoke up.

"Stig, I'm not so young as I used to be and I could do with a handy lad to help dig taters and seed the cabbages. Young Stok looks strong enough to me. Mrs. Craw would be only too glad to make over some of my old hand-me-downs for him and knit him a pair of socks and set out an extra place for him at our table."

"But he's my right hand, Maister Craw. And a fine woodcutter he'll be."

"That's as may be, but from what I've seen of the lad, he looks none too happy about it. He's much more comfortable grubbing about in the soil. Many's the time when you've been in The Wild Green Man I've given him a penny for picking caterpillars off my lettuces. Now, what is more, I've a spare parcel of land down the bottom of town. It's good fine ground; rich, and well-tilled, and it's a-waiting a lad that's of a mind to marry one day—if he comes to stay with me. It's not every young lad as could boast of a living like that. What do you say, Stig?"

Before Stig could answer, a woman called out. "How about Widow Cray, that's been bedridden these past three years?" she said. "That Hilsa of yours is a fine bonny lass that could look after her in return for bed and board. And that cottage would make a fine inheritance for a young girl of marriageable age. If she worked for Widow Cray five days a week, she could come up and see you on the other two. What do you say, Stig?"

Practically scratching his head off by now, Stig looked at Maister Craw, and the woman, then around at the rest of them. They all looked eager enough and no mistake.

Children were scarce around Clack just then, you see. But while Stig should have felt glad that the children were being offered good homes down in the town, where they would be properly clothed and fed and taught the decent way to live, yet he felt sad, too, for he loved every one of them and enjoyed their help and company. And then there was the baby. Stig would miss that one the most, for he reminded him so much of the Wife. But how could Stig stand in the baby's way when such a grand future awaited him down in the town?

He sighed and said, "I'll bring them down tomorrow." Then he went back up the mountainside singing a tune of sorts.

*   *   *

That night he talked to Hilsa and Stok when the others had gone to bed.

Stok looked unhappy. "I don't want to leave you, Father. I want to stay here and help you," he said, but Stig, watching the boy's eyes at the mention of the land, had seen the gleam in them.

"You're a good lad, and loyal, and well meaning. But you'll be better off down there, and Hilsa too, with all the rest."

"No, Father," Hilsa said. "I can't leave you. Who'll cook for you and clean for you and mend your clothes that you're always making holes in? I'd rather be here, looking after you than down there."

Stig hugged her to him. "Lass," he said. "You're growing faster than honeysuckle. In no time you'll have a mind to wed. Then where will I be?" He smiled. "Right back where I was before the Wife came, and I was right enough then." The smile wobbled a bit, then righted itself. The idea of being alone in the hut again seemed intolerable, but he'd have to get used to it, for the children's sake.

"That Widow Cray," he said, "needs someone like you to care for her. And think—you can keep an eye on your brothers and sisters for me, like. Five days a week only and you can come back up here the other two, if you've a mind. Please, Hilsa. It pains me as much as you, but up here is no life for a young girl. So what do you say?"

"Oh, Father," Hilsa cried, and laying her hand on her father's chest, she wept.

* * *

Down the children went the next day, four boys and five girls, scrubbed and shining, their clothes neatly patched, their hair brushed and braided. And on their best behavior. No crying, no sulking, and no feeling sorry for yourselves or no one will take you, Hilsa had told them, not least herself.

When at last it was time to go, thanks to Hilsa, the younger ones were all cheered up, even excited, for they loved to visit the town and the thought of actually living down there was beginning to sound like fun. Even Horvin did a hop and a skip or two and shouted down over the treetops with the rest to hear the echoes shatter and die away.

The new baby lay chuckling and gurgling in the Wife's crocheted blanket on top of the cart, while the rest scampered around Stig's heels, running on ahead and back again.

When they arrived, Hilsa bade her father goodbye and went off to Widow Cray's cottage.

"Goodbye, Hilsa," Stig called after her. "See you in three days' time!"

Stok embraced Stig and went off down the street with

Maister Craw, trying not to look too eager about it, Stig suspected.

As for the rest, they were snatched up—even fought over—and in no time were gone to new homes that wanted for children with scarcely time for a fare-you-well to Stig: all of them, that is, save for the baby still lying in the cart.

For while the women had fought for a look at him— thinking, as Stig had thought, that the new baby would be the best prize—they had each no sooner pulled aside the cover and seen his face than they'd fought to back off again. And though a number of the women were left empty-handed, they went off down the street, every one of them, looking anywhere but in the baby's direction.

One woman, though, desperate enough for a child of her own, did turn back and offer halfheartedly to take him.

Stig looked down at the baby in the cart, and ruffled up his own hair.

Then he leaned over, picked up the tiny wriggling thing in his great strong arms, and held it to him. So like the Wife. Down inside the blanket, next to the baby's chest lay the Wife's rune. "Thank you, but this one just came for the ride."

At this, as though he had understood, the new baby chuckled loudly. "Gom," he gurgled, and landed a tiny bony fist right in his father's eye. "Gom, Gom, Gom."

"Oh," the woman said, and went away leaving Stig standing with the baby by the cart.

"Well," Stig said to the baby. "If that's the way they feel. As for you, if you insist, Gom it is. Gom Gobble-chuck. 'Tis a fine name, and it suits you well, happy fellow that you are, laughing and chuckling all the while. It fair does my heart good to hear you. Come on, Gom, let's get ourselves back home." Stig settled Gom back into the cart, and hefting the shafts for the long haul up the trail, he moved at a brisk pace, singing loudly all the way.

Summer's gone: a bright and short-lived bubble,
The cattle huddle in their hay-warm stalls;
Chill mists wilt the cornfield's brittle stubble
And seasoned logs lie tidy by the walls.

Sheep crop close the autumn fallow;
Smoke coils up from every homely hearth;
Gone are swift and tiny darting swallow,
And badger, fox, and vole are gone to earth.

While way up high by wind-scored rock and pine,
Together Stig and Gom sit snug and warm:
And though around them shrill gales scream and whine,
There they'll stay content and safe from harm.

* * *

Time passed.

Down in the town, Gom's brothers and sisters grew; tall and broad as their father had before them, while the grown-ups grew older—as grown-ups tend to do, some with grumbling, some with resignation—those "not-getting-any-younger"s and "can't-complain-I-suppose"s that grown-ups love to use.

But Gom?

He grew some . . . then stopped. But small as he was, he learned to wield an axe, for wasn't he to be Clack's woodcutter one day?

This everyone took for granted, even Gom himself, until one summer morning in his tenth year, he wandered down by the creek. . . .

II

CHAPTER SEVEN

OM LAY UNDER the hot sun, leaning out over the edge of the creek. Directly below him, under the shadow of his head, a round smooth rock poked up out of the water. About it darted amber damselflies, their brisk wings whirring in the humid heat. Water striders walked the glassy surface, and deep down in the muddy depths dark shapes hung motionless, sheltering from the midday glare.

All these things Gom saw and heard yet he listened and watched some more, for there was one sound missing. Presently, he sat up and made a peculiar sound in the back of his throat, not high, not low, but in between; a sound that went something like, *glug-glung*. He sat quite still, as though waiting for a reply, but none came. "Funny," he muttered. "Where can he have got to?" Every morning without fail that summer old Leadbelly had taken his breakfast off that rock. Gom had been right around the creek, calling, and asking about him, but nobody had seen him; neither Bullfrog, nor Leadbelly's fellow tree frogs, nor Muskrat, nor even Water Moccasin, Gom was sure, though that snake would have swallowed Leadbelly in an instant and without a second thought and never tell—given the chance.

But nobody, not even Water Moccasin could catch old Leadbelly, for that frog was much too old and smart to let himself get caught by anyone. So the question remained, where was he?

Gom stared down at the bright water, fixing his eyes on the glare without blinking, hoping to bring on one of the waking dreams that came to him from time to time: a vision of Leadbelly, that would show him where the creature was and what he was doing. But all he got was the promise of a headache. He might have known. Those visions came only of their own sweet will, and seldom when he needed them.

He bent down and swished water over his head to take away the ache, then raked his fingers through his stiff, unruly thatch, pulling it back from his face, not that it would stay there when it dried.

It was not like Leadbelly to be missing. He was such a creature of habit. In a little while the air above the creek would be swarming with mosquitoes and midges, special favorites of his, and he always had such an appetite. Maybe, Gom told himself doubtfully, he was off on some private caper that couldn't wait.

But whatever the cause of Leadbelly's disappearance, if he didn't show up soon, Gom would have to wait to find it out, for the next day Gom was to take the weekly trip down into Clack with Stig.

That trip he thought of with mixed feelings.

He liked to visit with his married sister, Hilsa, in her cottage that used to be Widow Cray's, even if she was too busy nowadays to spend much time with him, what with the new baby and all. And Stok always had a word with him, out by Maister's Craw's vegetable patch.

And the rest of his brothers and sisters didn't mind him. In fact, they hardly paid him attention at all, so far apart they'd grown over the years.

Except for Horvin. Every time Gom went into Clack, Horvin stirred up the townschildren against him, and made trouble for him, if he could.

Gom leaned down to look at his face in the water.

Horvin called him ugly. *Rat-face.* Actually, Gom thought rats looked rather fine. He touched his nose where it bent at the bridge. Rats didn't have bent noses, nor did they have moles on the end of their chins as Gom had. Three, to be exact. Was he ugly? He must be, if Horvin said so. But he didn't feel ugly. Folk said he took after his mother, the Wife, and nobody ever called her ugly, least-ways, not in his hearing. He'd wanted to ask Stig about it for the longest time, but he dared not, for fear of making him angry again.

Once, Stig had overheard Horvin calling Gom ugly, and that was the one and only time Gom had ever seen his father out of countenance.

"As you are your mother's son," Stig said to Horvin, not raising his voice but making Gom shiver all the same, "don't let me ever hear you say that again. Gom is the im-age of the Wife, your mother, that reared you faithfully un-til as I've always told you, she had to go off on business of her own. She were small, she'd not come above halfway up my chest, and Gom looks fair to being the same, but she weren't ugly, don't you ever think it. When you abuse Gom so, you offer your mother like insult—and children who do that aren't worth a pinch of salt!"

Of course, this hadn't endeared Gom to his elder brother any the more. Horvin had gone off, his fist to his nose, looking at Gom in a meaningful way that Gom couldn't fail to understand.

"How that boy can say such things to you, his own brother, is beyond me," Stig said on their way home. "It's not natural, not natural at all. I just don't understand it."

But Gom did.

For another time—on Gom's eighth birthday, to be exact—Horvin had said and done something that Gom would never tell of aloud as long as he lived. Not to Stig, or Hilsa, or Stok, or anyone.

Gom was going through a back alley on his way to visit Hilsa and Stok for cake and a gift from each when Horvin, fourteen and almost as big as Stok already, had come up behind him, and seizing the leather thong around Gom's neck, had pulled it tight enough to choke him.

"Dwarf," he said. "Ugly, ugly dwarf. Nobody picked you to live with them. That's why you live with Father. Not because he wants you. Because no one else would take you, so there!"

Gom braced himself. He had heard it all before. And even though Stig had told him differently so many times, it still hurt. "Not true," he said. And with that, he kicked out at Horvin to make him let go.

Horvin let out a howl of rage but hung on all the same. "Dwarf dwarf evil dwarf!" he yelled. "It's all because of you that our mother left us!"

That was new. Gom, putting his hand to the small black pendant, tried to pull away. "It's not true! You're telling lies!"

"It is so, true." Horvin put his face close to Gom's and hissed. "It is, because I heard. I heard Father telling her that if she had one more child she'd have to go away, and then you were born. You're a curse, you know that? A curse that sent our mother away from us. That's why you're so ugly and small. Because you're a curse, a curse! Nobody wanted you. Nobody! You're the one that Father should have gotten rid of, not her!"

In a sudden burst of strength, Horvin stripped the thong from around Gom's neck and started up the alley, swinging the pendant around and around like a sling. But he hadn't gone many steps when suddenly he stumbled and fell, twisting his ankle under him, and the small black stone flew from his hand to land back at Gom's feet.

"Ow!" Horvin cried. "There! You see that? You did that! You put a wicked spell on it! Dwarf, dwarf, evil dwarf, just wait till I get my hands on you!"

Gom snatched up the pendant and went for his life, around the houses to hide in a barn. And as he crouched there, he felt the pendant tingling in his hand. It hadn't frightened him, but rather had comforted him somehow. There he stayed all that day holding the small black stone, feeling its vibrations, thinking over and over what Horvin had said; not crying, not moving, just lying there until it was time to go home, while Stig and Hilsa and Stok and a few other willing bodies searched for him from one end of the town to the other.

A curse, Horvin had called him. That had made his mother go away.

Back home on the mountain, Stig put him to bed, thinking him to be coming down with something, but Gom never said what really had ailed him.

He put his hand inside his tunic, drew out the pendant and turned it over and over in his hands, feeling its smooth warmth. It was "sleeping" just right now, as he put it, in the times when he couldn't feel anything. He put it to his ear, as always hoping to hear humming or some such sound, but he heard nothing.

His mother's rune, Stig called it. Her secret charm that she'd left with Gom the day he was born. Because, yes, it was true, he'd learned it from Stig himself, and from Hilsa and Stok, that she had gone off and left them all on that very day, just as Horvin had said. Was the rest of what his brother had said true as well? Not according to Stig. "With you she left it, special, to keep care of, like. Not with any of the others. Not with me, even. Just between you and me, boy, you understand?—you're the child she was really after, much as she loved the rest."

This Stig told him, every time they talked of the rune, and Gom tried really hard to believe him, in spite of what Horvin had said, and sometimes he did, though a question popped out from the back of his head sooner or later to make him doubt again.

If he was the child his mother had really wanted, *why had she gone off and left him the moment he was born?*

He stood up and moved away from the edge of the creek, remembering Leadbelly. Two hours to go to what his father called "elevenses," although they always had them nearer noon. Time enough to look for the frog.

Passing Gom on her way down to the creek was a large brown turtle.

Stooping, Gom rapped her shell in greeting. "Good morning. I don't suppose you've seen Leadbelly today?" he asked. Without answering, she ambled on toward the water, oblivious to anything but her own private dreamings.

A little way back from the bank, in a sandy hole, lay

a clutch of white eggs, barely covered over. The turtle's, Gom bet. Fresh laid and forgotten already, the absent-minded old thing.

A snake slid by. On a sudden impulse, Gom squatted over the eggs, hiding them, wafting his warm human scent over the sand that cradled them.

"Good day, Snake," Gom said. "You are in a rush."

"Greetings," the snake hissed. "Mustn't stop. Just felt Turtle's scratchings thisaways. That means eggs, and I'm so keen for sustenance."

"That's good. Well, happy hunting," Gom said. "So long."

So many eggs the snakes have had of turtles these past years. I do like to see fair play, Gom thought, as the snake slithered off.

He certainly did. He never told squirrels where their fellows hid nuts; or foxes of the fern beds where mallards hatched their broods, of the bramble brakes where pheasants reared their chicks, and of the hollow logs where 'possums nursed their young, though he knew them all.

On he went, over the mountain, asking every creature he met if it had seen or heard sign of Leadbelly, but without success. He tried all the familiar places along the stream flowing into the creek, right up to the entrance to the limestone caverns. He even put his head inside and called to Sessery, Wind's drafty cousin who blew about the passages deep within, but if she heard him, she didn't reply.

He was just turning away, when he noticed something bright lying beneath a boulder close beside him. Kneeling, he gingerly removed dead grass and dirt and there, on the ground, was the skeleton of a leaf, a brilliant yellow leaf, its delicate ribs gleaming in the sunlight like a strange metal.

Gom slipped his hand under it, eased it up, his eyes wide with wonder.

A golden loder leaf. A perfect skeleton.

Such a rare, precious find.

He took from a back pocket a flat box with neat wooden hinges and a cunning catch that he'd made himself that past winter, laboriously and at times somewhat impatiently, under Stig's watchful eye.

There! The leaf just fitted inside. Gom replaced the box in his back pocket, and went on. And on, and on. The farther he went, the more anxious he grew about the missing frog, so anxious that he didn't notice how far he'd gone from his regular haunts. Before he knew it, he was round the far side of the mountain, and out of bounds, and standing beneath a tall dead pine whose bark had been stripped clean off by lightning.

Atop the pine a mockingbird sat scolding him.

The instant Gom looked up, the bird shot up vertically a few feet, then dove, wings wide, back onto his perch, threatening Gom the while in cardinal, jay, blackbird, crow, robin, finch, and starling. Gom observed this multilingual maneuver several times more with interest.

"I can take a hint," he said at last. "But I haven't come to steal your backyard. I'm looking for Leadbelly, a small green tree frog. Have you any idea where I might find him?"

The bird executed another vertical loop before he spoke, this time in his own voice. "Down, down, down, down," he called, then hopped about.

Gom looked the way the bird was facing.

Below the pine was a deep gully, dark and cold and still unlit by the bright morning sun.

"Down there? But why?" Why would Leadbelly go down there?

Just then, he heard the faint sound of running water.

Gom nodded. Leadbelly, the homebody, had never left the creek until that summer, when he befriended Gom, and even now ventured abroad only from the safety of Gom's shoulder. But he'd well grow brave to the point of folly if driven by hunger or lured by the promise of a rare and special feast. "Down there? You say the frog's down there?" he asked the mockingbird. In answer, the bird shot upward and this time flew away.

Gom stared over the edge of the gully. It didn't look very inviting. But if Leadbelly could make it, so could he. He began to climb down.

CHAPTER EIGHT

E FOUND THE GOING rough.
The gully side was so slippery
and apt to crumble. Careful as Gom was, he started grit
and gravel tumbling, so that as he moved down it fell
after him, showering him with fine dust and sharp stone
chips that lodged inside his collar.

Halfway down Gom stopped, and looking upward to
the early morning sky, realized for the first time how far
off the beaten track he'd come. He thought of his father
working away on the other side of the mountain, secure in
the belief that his son was down by the creek. Maybe, Gom
thought uncomfortably, he ought to go back. Stig had forbidden him this far side of the mountain on account of its
being, in his words, "too traitorous to mess around in." But,
Gom thought, picking out some of the chips from his collar, there were other places, too, that Stig forbade him, much
closer to home. Places where Gom still went often. Like

the limestone caverns, which were to Gom as safe as Clack's main street—though his father would never believe that. Stig worried about him so; why, Gom told himself, he didn't know. But he did, really.

"That nose of yours," Stig would say to him. "You up and follow it at the crack of a twig without ever stopping to see where it's taking you."

Gom looked down. He'd come so far. It would be a waste to turn back.

He moved on.

* * *

The gully bottom was even darker and colder than it had seemed from above. And strangely hushed. Except for the sound of running water.

Gom moved out cautiously until he came upon a sudden stream rushing along the gully. He looked around, cleared his throat, and called. *Glinger—lugger linger-lug!* ("Leadbelly—it's me, Gom!")

Silence, save for the echoing gurgle of water.

Gom walked with the current a little way until the stream disappeared into a sudden hole. He stopped. If Leadbelly had taken that route, there was no way Gom could follow him. He turned back upstream until he came upon a basin, a small round waterhole looking up at him like a great dark eye.

Gom knelt and leaned out over it.

Glung. Glung. Gligger-lung! ("Leadbelly—Leadbelly, answer me!")

Still there was no reply.

"Bother," Gom said to himself. "What if he's down there and can't hear me? I wish I could see."

At that moment, the sun, slicing the treetops, hit the pool, turning blind black water to light translucent green. A green alive with whirligigs and caddis-fly larvae, more of Leadbelly's favorite food. Gom smiled. The frog had likely learned of this place, come and taken in a bellyful and rolled aside somewhere to sleep it off.

Gom was just getting up to go and look for him when a glint of something deep down in the water caught his eye and held it; a host of shining yellow flecks churning like so many tiny bright fish trapped in the cold currents.

Gom watched, fascinated, wondering what they were, and where they had come from. He'd certainly seen nothing like them round the other side of the mountain. Were they from higher up, washed down by the water?

He moved upstream a pace or two, searching intently, until he spied more of the bright golden flecks caught by the stream's gravel bed, on their way to the waterhole. He knelt down, lifted one out, and set it on the tip of his finger, turning it this way and that to catch the sunlight. It was a flake of yellow metal about the size of his small fingernail.

He rubbed the flake on his sleeve to shine it up some more. It bent, and broke. Gom dropped the bits back into the water. Wouldn't be much good for an axe blade, he thought. But if the flakes were not useful, they certainly were pretty. He fished out another, polished it gingerly on his sleeve, and held it out. How fine it looked; such a bright warm yellow. Like the golden loder leaf he'd found outside the limestone caverns.

He took out the little wooden box, opened it, and compared the leaf and the flake side by side. The flake was brighter and shinier, but the leaf in its perfection was the finer and more rare.

Unique.

Still, Gom could not deny that the flake was an interesting find. And he would dearly love to ask his father about it but he didn't see how, without telling him where he'd found it.

He carefully stowed the leaf away again, then, sighing, held the flake out over the stream to drop it back, but at the last minute he couldn't bring himself to let it go. Instead, he opened a small pouch hanging from his belt and slipped the flake inside.

Then, curious to trace the flakes to their source, he moved on upstream a short distance until he was halted by sheer mountain wall. At his feet, the stream gushed from a ragged hole with tremendous force.

Gom felt a surge of excitement.

What a wonderful morning! His search for Leadbelly had turned up first the golden leaf, then the strange flakes, and now, find of finds, Sessery's back door. Her *secret* back door, for she'd never told him about it, and he'd certainly never seen it from the inside.

Gom squatted beside the frothing, foaming water. Where did the stream hit the rock back in there, and why had he never found it? He thought he'd explored every passage, on every level under the mountain, right through to this far side. Obviously he was wrong. He stared unblinking at the endless arc of glittering spray until a peculiar buzzing started in the back of his head, and everything went dark.

Gom's excitement deepened. On top of everything else, he was about to have one of his waking dreams! He closed his eyes and squeezed his hands together, waiting for bright pictures to form—brighter and more vivid than ordinary dreams, brighter than the real world.

All remained dark for a while. Then, at his feet in the dark, yellow specks began to glow and waver, big as turtle's eggs this time: lumps of golden light, lying in shallow water.

Gom was just bending down to pick one up when the air before him began to fill with radiance, a rich warm, amber glow shedding its light onto the golden pieces. As Gom looked into the light it seemed to him that at its center, just for a moment, shone a man's face . . . or was it? Weren't those dark holes eyes, and nostrils, and wasn't that a mouth? Gom caught his breath. For the flash of an instant the face vanished, dissolved almost, leaving nothing but bare gleaming bone. Why—it was a skull! Gom swallowed. He'd never seen a human skull before. Only the bones of animals, about the mountain forest.

Almost before he could register what he'd seen, the skull was gone, and the glow, leaving the golden lumps shining in the darkness at his feet. He bent down to pick one up, but as he bent they vanished also and he felt the hot sun on his eyelids once more.

He sat down and leaned his back against the warm cliff face, feeling dizzy and a little weak. Then as his head began to clear, he became aware of the rune tingling against his chest, so powerfully it almost pained him. He drew it out, and put it to his ear, but all he heard was water bursting from the mountain wall.

Gom kept his eyes shut for a while, feeling the stone's vibrations. Had they to do with his vision? He'd not felt them during other waking dreams. But what had the vision meant? That the lumps were under the mountain, that he was invited to seek them there? By whom? The skull? He wasn't sure that he'd seen one, now. It had all been so quick. Those lumps, though, were a different matter. They'd been clear enough, shining at his feet. He sat up. If he was being invited under the mountain, was the rune telling him to go—or warning him to stay away?

He got to his feet. The stone was quiet again, its sudden energy spent; gone, like the vision. There was nothing now to prove that he had ever seen the amber light, and the skull, and the shining golden pieces.

No matter, thought Gom. He had, and that was enough. And now the excitement of discovery was upon him. All thought of Leadbelly was gone. And of getting back to Stig. He certainly couldn't leave without taking a look through the mountain wall. But how? Not through that hole, not for anything! Heights never bothered him, nor depths. He could climb steep cliffs and travel deep tunnels without a second thought. But water? While his father swam across the creek every night, going under all the way across and back again, Gom could never bring himself to follow. The most he could manage was to take a deep breath, pinch his nose and duck his head into the wash bucket at the side of the hut each morning, and even that set him gasping and dabbing at his smarting eyes. "Father," he'd say, "if we were meant for water, we'd have fins and gills. As it is, we have feet to walk the dry land and lungs to breathe the air!"

He put his face to the ground and examined the base of the rock cliff in front of him. Beside the torrent, hidden by the rock overhang, was a narrow slit wide as a thin smile. Did the slit go all the way inside, and was there enough room for a small body to squeeze through?

Gom picked up a dry branch, sticky with resin, from the gully floor and thrusting it into the slit, jiggled it about. Then he gave it a sharp push. It went clear through and landed with a slight clatter on the other side.

After a moment's hesitation, Gom squirmed through

after it, scraping his shoulders painfully on the overhang. The slit narrowed. Back, he told himself. You're going to get stuck, and then what will you do? Your father will never find you here. On, he argued. You'll never forgive yourself if you turn back now.

He squeezed and pushed and wriggled.

At last with a gasp and a grunt he rolled out onto a cold wet floor. Was he now truly inside the mountain? Or was this but a sort of back hallway? He stood up and fished out his tinder box. With this he set the brand alight and at once the space around him filled with fragrant smoke, then light.

He was standing in a low tunnel, so low that it scraped his head. Down the middle of it raced the deep stream. On Gom's side of it, a narrow ledge—the floor on which he stood—curved away out of sight. On the other side of the tunnel, rock wall ran sheer down into the water with not so much as a toehold in sight. He stroked the rock with his fingertips. Not limestone. This stuff was dark gray, almost black. It was also harder, sharper, than limestone, and it glistened with myriads of tiny stars like the flagstones in the hut. He was on a different level from the limestone tunnels, he decided. A lower one, because Sessery's front door was higher, much higher up the mountain on the other side.

After a second's hesitation, he started up the tunnel, the torchlight glistening off the starry walls, shining gold on black ripples beneath.

But that was the only gold that he could see by the light of the torch. He wondered then if it was getting late. Maybe he should go back now, and come again another day. It must be time for elevenses, and he hadn't seen sign of Leadbelly. And here he was, gadding about on a wild goose chase after strange amber lights, skulls, and shining golden lumps. He must have a touch of the sun! He turned to go back. Then turned again.

The stream was deep. The lumps had been lying in shallow water. Like a pool. Just a few more steps and you might find it, he told himself. Another minute won't make all that much difference.

In less than that Gom came out into a low, wide cavern. Its floor, almost entirely flooded, formed a backwater left by the tiny torrent in its rush to reach outside.

How deep was it, he wondered? He bent down, lowering the flaming brand the better to see, and there they were, the bright lumps poking up out of the shallow water, just as they'd been in his dream. He straightened up, waiting for the warm amber glow. It didn't come. Pity, for he was sure that the vision had meant something. Still hoping for a sign, a clue, or something more to happen, he moved about, waving the torch this way and that. No. There was no skull in that small cavern, glowing or otherwise.

Only the shining lumps lying like golden eggs at his feet. He stooped, picked one up, put it in his pocket to show Stig. Took it out again, and threw it back into the pool. He could no more tell his father about the lumps than he could about the flakes. Not that day, anyhow. He would have to keep this find, and his excitement, to himself.

He hurried back up the tunnel, worked his way out through the rock slit, and ran back to the basin. After one last look at the roiling flakes he scrambled up the gully side, until he reached the blasted pine.

Its top perch was still bare.

"I'll bet Leadbelly never was here," Gom told himself disgustedly. "Such a sense of humor that mockingbird had, having himself a joke at my expense." On second thought, he smiled. "But I found such wonders down there today that the jest worked to my favor in the end. I must remember to thank that wretched bird when I see him next!"

Gom hurried back around the mountain by the way he'd come.

But rushed as he was, he didn't go far before he stopped short. His keen eyes had spotted a strange creature clinging to a low tree-branch. It was long and spindly, with a tiny head and enormous front legs folded up in the air like human arms. A praying mantis, it was, of the same bright green of the tree and crouched so still that it was all but invisible.

But not to Gom.

He took the mantis, cupped it carefully in his hands, and ran on to where his father was, feeling very pleased. Stok had been having trouble with bugs in the cabbage patch lately, and Gom had a mind to help him out. The mantis stirred, lightly tickling his palm. "Not long," he told the insect. "You'll soon have a big jar to share with three more of your kind—though I'll have to divide you off so's you won't fight. Tomorrow you and your fellows will go down into the town where you can eat to your hearts' content."

* * *

His father had almost finished his elevenses. "I was just coming to look for you, son," he said. "What have you there?"

Gom opened out his hands.

"Aha!" Stig said, nodding fondly. "I might have knowed it."

Gom put the mantis in the jar with the three others, went to sit by his father, and picked up his slab of bread and cheese. His helping was generous—too generous. There hadn't been much left in the larder. He had to watch Stig always, or he'd go short on the food he needed to do his heavy work, in order to feed his son. Clothes they never wanted for, even if the fit wasn't always quite right, for the townswomen were ever ready with hand-me-downs for both of them. But, as Gom had early learned, the merchants enjoyed the hassle of the barter trade, and getting the better of a deal was their chief sport.

However, as Gom had also found out, Stig had neither head nor stomach for the game. This pained Gom. "Father," he'd say, the times their food store ran out before town day, "hunger is not a game. You must tell those people fair and square when they bid you short."

Stig would nod, and agree with him, but things never changed. The real trouble was, as Gom saw it, that his father so disliked fuss that he'd rather go hungry than complain.

So Gom had decided to watch out for them both.

He cut for himself little tally sticks, one for the butcher, one for the blacksmith, one for the greengrocer, and so on. On these he kept count, by notching them with his knife, how many pounds or jars or bags of whatever food they'd gotten each week, and from whom, for what wood and for how many logs of it.

Stig had seemed very pleased with his ingenuity. "Why, I'm that glad you've learned to keep count so well. Just as long as you keep them sticks to yourself, I can't see the harm. But remember—the folks down below are real kind to us in lots of other ways, so we'll let a little close bartering go by, and turn a blind eye, for peace's sake, eh son?"

Gom had agreed, but not very happily. Time and again he stood by and watched the townsmen chisel them out of good value. One of these days he was afraid he'd forget himself and let his tongue get the better of him.

He took a bite of his sandwich. "Did you have enough to eat, Father?"

"Yes, son." Stig nodded to the mantis jar. "Funny how quiet they sit in there," he said. "It's like you've told them what good times they're going to have."

Gom laughed.

"You might well laugh," Stig said. "But often enough I've said, I swear you speak to the critters out here—and they talk back to you!"

Gom munched on. He was sure that he'd gotten his own love for animals from Stig. So it had surprised him the day he realized that his father couldn't understand a word they said. For he himself had understood them as plain as can be since he could remember. "Tell me again, Father," he said. "About finding me with those blue jays."

"Oh that." Stig took a drink of water. Then he sighed with contentment and settled back against the tree. "You were a real trial to me, you were, and you only a baby. One day I set you down on your blanket as your mother made, and I told you to stay put. Every five minutes or so I looked at you, and there you were, good as gold, watching an old ant crawling up a blade of grass. A moment later, you'd gone and did I ever have a time finding you! Drat the boy, I said, not meaning it, mind. That nose of his will get him into a right pickle some day."

Gom laughed, a little more loudly than he needed to.

"Anyways, I upped and set about finding you and bringing you back. I finally spotted you sitting under a tree. Looking upwards you were, and smiling your face off. I was just about to pick you up when you let out a screech that fair set me back on my heels. It were a jay's call, or as near to one as any I've heard human make. And bless me if one didn't start up out of that tree above your head and answer you back. Why, I said, it just sounded as though you two were having a real old gossip! I picked you up and scolded you—only in jest, mind. I said, fine son you turn out to be, talking nineteen to the dozen with an old jaybird and you not even calling me 'Father' yet. With that you grabbed my nose and pulled it. 'Fa-ther,' you said. 'Father, Father, Father!' " Stig tilted back his head and laughed aloud. "But, say, where have you been all morning, son?" He nodded over to a pile of blackwood waiting to be stripped and chopped with Gom's small axe for kindling.

"Looking for Leadbelly," Gom said. "But I can't find him anywhere."

"Gone off on business of his own, that's what," Stig said. "He'll be back."

Gom ate the last of his bread and cheese, saying nothing. His father loved to hear all about his friends, but did he realize how deeply Gom cared for them? Gom wasn't sure. Those creatures were his only playmates, you see, and sadly, their lives were so brief and uncertain. So Gom had every cause to be worried about Leadbelly. About not being able to find him.

Remembering the flake, however, Gom cheered up a little. If only he could show it to his father . . . No. Better not. Instead, he brought out the golden loder leaf. It was, in any case, much the better find.

"My," Stig said, touching it lightly with his great finger. "It's perfect. Where did you find it?"

"Outside the limestone caverns. Under a rock pile, it was. I'd not have seen it if I hadn't been looking for Leadbelly. I didn't go in," he added quickly.

But he needn't have worried. Stig was still examining the fragile thing in wonder. "Just like your mother, you are, though I say it again and again. She were always doing the same. Picking up little treasures I'd never have noticed in a million years. She'd be right proud of you, if she knew."

Gom did not miss the sadness behind Stig's words, much as his father tried to hide it. His hand went to the rune. "Maybe she does know, Father," Gom said, then wondered at what he'd said.

Stig looked at him oddly for a moment, then he sighed. "Aye, maybe she does at that." He held up the leaf to the sun. "How bright it looks against the light!"

Like the flake in my pouch, thought Gom, and again was almost tempted to take it out and show his father, but once more he changed his mind. One forbidden place was enough for that day.

He took back the leaf, returned it to its box, and stowed it back in his pocket. I'll show him the flake another day, he thought. And tell him about the vision too. Perhaps. And perhaps not, for his father always tended to worry so. He jumped up, seized his axe, and set to work on the kindling wood with a will, and as he worked, he thought again of old Leadbelly. Oh well, he thought hopefully. Maybe I'll find him home in two days' time. But if he doesn't show up by then, I fear he never will.

CHAPTER NINE

T DAWN THE NEXT morning, Gom went down into town with Stig, the mantis jar wedged safely among the logs. The mist drifted as fine rain over the trail and dripped from the trees on either side. It promised to be a good hot day, all right, Stig said, and just to make sure, he sang about it, the whole of the way. And why not? As Stig often said, the way was always shorter for a song.

As they walked the last slope leading down into the main street, Gom's heart beat faster, and his fingers squeezed the tally sticks in his pocket.

"Now, son," Stig said, breaking off in the middle of a line, almost as though he'd sensed Gom's tightening. "Remember what I said about them sticks."

"Yes, Father," Gom said, looking down at his scuffed, downtrodden boots moving forward along the stony ground, one, two, one, two, but he kept his hand around the sticks all the same.

He shifted around to the far side of the cart. Maybe if he kept out of sight, he'd not be tempted to interfere. Young lads should be seen and not heard, the gaffers outside The Wild Green Man said often enough—and always looking at him. Maybe he should try it, to keep himself quiet.

Bok the butcher was waiting on his doorstep, talking with a customer.

"Mornin', Maister Stig. I'll take two stacks of the blackwood today to smoke the fresh hams that Farmer Trobbs sold me. Let's see . . . we agreed on two pounds of sausages and four bags of beef bones for that last time, didn't we?" He glanced to the man beside him with, Gom could swear it, a nod and a wink.

"Right." Stig, smiling broadly, hefted out the wood.

Gom's face went hot with indignation. Two pounds of sausages, indeed! Before he knew it, he'd stepped out from behind the cart. "Wrong." Avoiding his father's eye, he produced his tally sticks, picked out the one for the butcher, and studied the notches he'd cut in it. "It was *three* pounds of sausages, and *five* bags of beef bones—*and* a crock of lard—no, two, for I see that it's cheaper this week."

"Gom!" Stig said mildly. "After I told you, an' all!"

Bok bent down and put his square red face close to Gom's. "You're so sharp, cut your fingers on your own blade you will one day, mark my words." Scowling, the butcher went back into his shop.

"Or if he doesn't," the customer said, "Bok'll do it for him." With a laugh, he moved off down the street.

"Well. That's a fine start we've made to the day, son. I think you'd better take yourself off for a while," Stig said, but Gom stood his ground.

Bok, muttering, came back out and handed over sausages, bones, and dripping under Gom's watchful eye. "You bring that boy up too loose, Stig," he said when he'd done. "We don't like lip down here."

"Oh, don't mind him, Maister Bok," Stig said, obviously trying to excuse Gom, which made Gom angrier still. "He's but a lad. He means no disrespect, do you Gom?"

"No, I don't." Gom faced the angry butcher defiantly. "I just like to see fair play, that's all."

"Fair play! Well, of all the—" Bok's face went a deeper red. "Can't a man make a simple mistake once in a while?"

"Yes, he surely can, if there's no one to mind him. But you needn't worry about that anymore," Gom replied, knowing he shouldn't, yet unable to stop himself now. He held up the tally stick and shook it. "My father has agreed to let me keep count for us."

Bok's mouth fell open. "Well, of all the—" he cried.

Gom dodged back out of range behind his father, on the far side of the cart. Stig said goodbye, picked up the cart shafts, and rumbled on up the street until they were out of earshot. There, Stig stopped and looked down at Gom sadly. "Son," he said, "I told you plain as plain I wanted no trouble, and here you go stirring it up. It's too bad."

"Sorry, Father," Gom said. "I'll try not to do it again. But you'll still let me keep tally, won't you?"

Stig nodded slowly. "Aye, son. I suppose so. For I know as how you mean well, and I'm right proud for you to practice your numbers. But watch your step from now on, you understand?"

Gom nodded, and they moved on to Maister Craw's greengrocery. There he stayed behind the cart, while his father swapped wood for cabbages, and tomatoes, and green beans, and corn. Never mind, he consoled himself, as Craw bid his father down at every turn. I took care of Bok today. Perhaps in time, Father will let me have a bigger say.

At Crick & Son, the potters', Stig got them new blue soup bowls to replace their old cracked ones in return for good oak kiln wood. As Gom passed Wendle, the shoemaker's, he looked down at his boots and sighed. The soles of his boots were so thin that he could feel the round street cobbles pressing up through them. Both he and Stig needed new footwear, but Wendle's prices were so high all they could afford was to have them mended again and again until the uppers were too weak to take any more repairs.

When at last they reached The Wild Green Man, Gom left Stig there to enjoy his elevenses and ran off with the mantis jar down the street and through one of the alleyways to a tiny cottage inside a neat white fence. He pushed open the gate and trod the little brick path fragrant with mint, past clumps of snapdragon and sweet william, daisies and scarlet roses. He paused for a moment to admire the bright pretty colors, sniffing in deeply the strong sweet scents, so different from the green and earthy smells of the mountainside. Then he went on to the small front door. There, he set down the jar beside the step, and standing on tiptoe, raised the round brass knocker and let it fall three times.

"Who is it? Who's there?" A young woman's voice; warm, motherly.

"It's me, Hilsa. Gom."

The door opened a crack onto a dim little kitchen from which wafted a fine rich smell of baking.

"Why, Gom! Come you in here quick and shut the door behind you, there's a good lad. The seedcake's in the oven. One draft through that door and it won't rise. Now: let's see how much you've growed this week."

Hilsa set her baby on her hip and with a floury hand took Gom's chin and tilted his face up for her to see, which she always did, to Gom's great discomfiture. "Why, you're not a hair bigger! What is Father feeding you? A young lad like you should be shooting up like a weed. Here."

Hilsa pointed to the scrubbed tabletop. "Take one. Mind the tray, it's still hot."

Gom took, and Hilsa laughed. "The biggest one, as usual. You know, Father should let you come to stay with me for a while and then we'd see how fast you'd grow. Like Gudy here. Gudy—" She bounced the fat pink baby still at her hip. "Say hello to Uncle Gom." She lifted the baby and put it close to Gom's face.

The baby looked startled for a moment, then began to wail.

"Now, now, Gudy. It's only Gom." Hilsa jiggled the baby vigorously. "For shame carrying on so! Don't take it ill, Gom, dear. He's like that with everybody right now, even his own father. It's his teeth growing in. Here, Gudy, show Uncle Gom your teeth."

In answer, Gudy bawled some more. Hilsa was right. There were two teeth, Gom saw. Shining like tiny budding stalactites in the cavern of Gudy's mouth.

Gom broke his hotcake in two.

"Here," Hilsa said, "let's have some honey on that." She took a large earthenware pot out of her cupboard and ladled rich amber honey onto the hotcake. "Don't get up," she said. "Take your time and don't mind me. But I've got to get about my work. I'm that behind. I still have the wash to do."

"I'll help you, Hilsa," Gom said. "I'll help you scrub."

"Thank you, Gom, but I'm halfway through."

"Then I'll hang it out for you."

"That's nice of you, Gom dear, but if I let down the clothesline for you to reach, the things'll trail in the dirt.

Tell you what—it's time for Gudy's morning sleep. How about singing him a song?"

"What song, Hilsa?"

"Oh, anything. Father sang us so many it's hard to pick but one."

While Gom finished his cake, she laid Gudy in the old owl cradle that Stig had brought down the mountain when he heard that the baby was coming.

"Good boy, Gudy. Sleep now for Mama," she said, and bending low, she tucked him in and kissed him.

Gom brushed the last of the crumbs from his mouth, knelt by the cradle and, rocking it, began to sing:

A finch and a sparrow once sat on a sill,
And bade one another good day.
The finch preened her feathers down with her bright bill.
And strutted, as proud as cock-jay.

"Brown sparrow," said finch, "pray, look your fill.
Don't you covet my colors so gay?"
"Why, no," said the sparrow, "not even a quill.
I much prefer plain brown and gray."

Said the finch to the sparrow, her voice rising shrill,
"You can't possibly mean what you say!"
"Yes, I do," said the sparrow, "for you'll be here still,
After I've gone and flown clean away!"

Hilsa came up behind him. "His eyes are still open," she said. "That were a strange song. Father never sang that one to us. I never heard it before."

Gom looked up at her. "Oh? Father sang it a lot to me. The Wife taught it to him."

"But Mother didn't sing. She told stories."

"The words were hers. He made up the tune."

"Oh," Hilsa said, nodding. "And that were right pretty. But not restful, like, for a baby to sleep to." She bent over and stroked Gudy's cheek. "You know, I still can't make sense of that song. I'm sure that any common brown sparrow would envy a finch, Gom. And why couldn't the finch fly away?"

"Because," Gom said earnestly, "the finch was in a cage."

"A cage?" Hilsa looked doubtful. "Then why didn't it say so?"

"You're supposed to guess. The finch is so beautiful and attractive that folk like to have her around, so they catch her and keep her close to them so that they can enjoy her company. But nobody wants the plain old brown sparrow. Which leaves her free to fly wherever she wants."

"Hmm. Well," Hilsa said, straightening up. "It were a right pretty tune, even if it weren't particularly restful, like. Sing another song, Gom. One to shut that darling rascal's eyes."

Gom started the cradle rocking again, and sang a favorite song of his father's about the wind lulling the mountain to sleep; stroking the grasses, soothing the leaves, smoothing out the waters, gathering the mist clouds about the peak like eiderdown. And as he sang, he heard Hilsa in the scullery, the comfortable sounds of cloth slapping about in the washtub. Gudy's eyelids wavered, then closed.

At last, Gom stood up and tiptoed through the kitchen into the tiny steam-laden scullery.

"He's gone off," he said. "Thanks for the hotcake, Hilsa."

Hilsa left her tub and took Gom in a warm, moist embrace.

"Bless you," she said. "Take another on your way out. And shut the door quiet behind you."

*   *   *

Chewing cake, Gom wandered along with the mantis jar to the end of the street until it petered out into a no-man's-land of bramble, and thistle, sweet nettles, and ripening cob-nuts.

Just beyond that, to the left, was Maister Craw's cabbage patch, and Gom's eldest brother, Stok, just twenty-two and working his tail off.

Stok straightened up, smiling.

"Mornin', little 'un. You've flour on your face. I know where you've been. What's up?"

Gom broke the cake in two and held it out.

Stok took the larger piece and popped it into his mouth. "That Hilsa, she makes the best oatcakes this side of Windy Mountain, but I'm blowed if I can wheedle a crumb out of her. Yet she always has one for you, eh?" And he ruffled up Gom's hair.

Gom held out the jar. Stok took it, peering through the glass.

"What's this, then?" he said. "Another one of your capers?"

Lifting the lid, Gom tipped the jar upside down over a nearby cabbage. "Whatever's been bothering your cabbages won't anymore, you'll see," he said. "They're hungry enough to take on five cabbage patches, and the rest of Maister Craw's field."

Stok looked down in amazement. So well did the mantises blend in with the purple-brown of the cabbage leaves that you'd hardly know they were there. "Well, I'll be—" he said. "I'd never have thought of that. You know, you really are clever in your odd fashion. Too clever for some folk around here, but I daresay you know that. Horvin's looking out for you, by the way."

Gom nodded. Horvin usually was. "What for this time?"

"He's made a new game and he's waiting for you to try it."

"What sort of game?"

Stok picked up his shirt, wiped his face on it. "He made me promise not to tell. But I can say as it'll make you good and mad—that is, if it's not all over and you're not too late."

"Too late?" Gom frowned. "For what?"

Stok turned away and picked up his spade again. "You go and see. He's a lout, is our Horvin, picking on a poor little green critter like that. I tried to get it from him, but he ran off too quick for me."

"Little green critter?" Gom's heart quickened.

"A frog. A little, fat, green tree frog." Stok pointed to the mantis jar. "He's got it shut up in a jar just like that one. It looks so hot, it does, with no water to sit in, and in a terrible way. Horvin can't wait to show it to you, the young rogue."

"Where is he?"

"On his front doorstep. Where else? Sitting around lazy as ever and not a decent stroke of work for anyone."

Gom began to run.

"Here—keep your head!" Stok called after him. "You'll only be dancing to his tune, else."

Gom went on to Horvin's house, moving at a clip.

CHAPTER TEN

ORVIN WAS SITTING on his front doorstep, a jar between his knees, an assortment of treasures at his feet. Around him squatted several townschildren, quite a bit younger than he. On seeing Gom, Horvin sat back and, cupping his hands around the jar, held it out toward him. Its lid, Gom saw, was pierced with little holes. "Gom! Want to win a treasure trove?" Horvin lifted his fingers off the jar to let Gom see through the glass.

Inside was a lump of mud.

Lung, went the mud. *Lung* and *glug-a-lug.*

Gom bent down. Leadbelly! He came up again, trying to look casual, trying not to show that he cared, for Leadbelly's sake. "It's only a tree frog," he said.

The children squealed derisively.

"Tell us, tell us! Gom, tell us what it said!"

"He said," Gom began, but they weren't listening, as he might have guessed. Why did he bother?

They took off, hopping around him, making gobbling sounds, imitating him, but not successfully.

"Quiet!" yelled Horvin. "Quiet, and listen." He fixed Gom with his round blue eyes. "Say something, Gom. Say something in frog."

"Oh, yes!" cried the rest of the children. "Do it, Gom! Do it!"

"All right." He had to anyway, to tell Leadbelly that all would be well; that he, Gom, would get him out and back up the mountain somehow.

Gom got down beside the jar, making low gobbling noises in his throat that sounded as though he'd swallowed old Leadbelly whole. The children laughed so wildly that Horvin could scarcely shut them up.

It was no use. Leadbelly wouldn't listen to him. The frog was half dead already from heat and lack of water. The children's cries, drowning Gom's voice, only made his cries more frantic.

"Oh, look, Horvin!" cried one small girl. "It's trying to get out! Tighten the lid, Horvin! Tighten the lid!"

Horvin snatched the jar from under Gom's nose and shook it violently, bouncing the frog off its sides until the little thing subsided, dazed.

"You didn't have to do that." Gom clenched his fists to hide his rage.

Horvin ignored him. "It's tight enough, Tilly. He'll not get out." He banged the jar back down on the ground then turned to Gom. "Well? Tell us what it said."

Gom considered. Leadbelly, totally dazed, could only babble about getting back to the creek. He was dying for water, and starving for midges and damselflies and whirligigs—but Horvin wasn't to know that. Luckily, before Leadbelly completely lost his head, he'd managed to tell Gom one important thing. Gom looked down at the trophies at Horvin's feet. "He said for me to ask you how you got all those."

Somebody snickered behind him.

"Shush," Horvin said. "Why does it want you to do that?"

Because, thought Gom, he'll die if he doesn't get out of there soon. He wants me to win him and take him back home. But all he said aloud was, "He says he wants some more exercise."

"Careful!" cried one of the boys, looking fierce. "They're up to something."

"They?" Horvin grinned derisively. "Come on, Dugan. Whoever heard of anyone talking to a frog!" Turning back to Gom, Horvin pointed to the objects piled up around his feet. "You want to know how I won these, Gobblechuck? Well, I won them with this here frog—and that there trench in my backyard. Game's called Pick a Spot, or All-or-Nothing. You mark a place anywhere in the trench, and I set the frog down on the starting line. The frog gets three jumps. If it hits your mark, you win all this. If it fails, then you lose, and you have to give something to me."

Gom stared down at the jar. Why, the frog could jump in any direction, and to any height. The chances of his landing on a specific spot were small indeed. Winning therefore depended completely on luck, and had nothing whatsoever to do with the frog's jumping skills. He looked around at the children's faces. Didn't they realize that this was but a gamble? That Horvin had all the odds? If they did, it made no difference. Horvin was their leader. It was Horvin's game, and he made the rules. Small wonder Horvin had won all that trash.

He looked at Leadbelly and grunted. The little frog sat up, raised his head. *Glug*, he went. *Glug-lung*.

"Sounds clear enough," Gom said. "Let's go."

"Not so fast." Horvin winked at the others. "I'll see your stake first."

"My what?"

"What you give me when you lose."

"But I won't lose."

When the laughter had died down, Horvin held out his hand.

"Your stake, or no contest."

Gom, following Horvin's glance, looked down at his chest—more particularly, at the middle button of his tunic under which lay the rune. Why, Gom realized with a shock. Horvin wanted it! But he'd never dare demand it, Gom would bet. Not after what happened on Gom's eighth birthday. But if not the rune, then what? He clearly had to find something. Gom fossicked around in his pockets and pulled out his wooden box. "How about this?" He raised the lid, and held it out.

Horvin stood up and looked inside, the rest crowding him. Then, disgustedly, he pushed the box away. "No go," he said. "Who wants an old leaf?"

"But it's a golden loder leaf," Gom insisted. "A perfect skeleton. Look. Not a vein broken, not a wrinkle, not a single scratch or crack. Don't you know how rare that is?"

"No I don't, and I don't want to. But I do know that a bit of old rubbish like that's of no use to me. Can you eat it? Or shoot birds with it? Or use it to catch a fish? No. You'll have to do better than that."

Gom thought for a moment or two, then went through his pockets again. "Here. How about this, then?" He brought out a small white object, oval in shape, shiny as glass, and light as thistledown.

Horvin took it suspiciously and turned it over. "Why, it's only a stone," he said, wrinkling up his nose and handing it back.

"It isn't so," Gom insisted. "Look again, Horvin."

Reluctantly, Horvin did so, seeing now the tiny insect embedded within: the minute horns protruding from an armored, horselike head; myriad legs frozen forever beneath a hairy thorax, and delicate, reticulated wings half spread as if poised to fly the glassy coffin that had sealed the creature in so suddenly. "I found this under an old hollow tree that Father cut down last fall. Deep in the roots, it was. Goodness knows how long it had been there."

Horvin wasn't impressed. "First a moldy old leaf, and now a bug. A bug, everyone. Look Tilly. Gom wants to trade me a measly old bug."

"A bug! A bug! Ugh! How disgusting!" Tilly pushed Horvin's hands away.

"It can't hurt you, Tilly," Gom said, taking the stone back. "It's been dead these thousand ages past, or so Sessery says."

"Sessery? Who's that when he's at home?" Horvin hadn't heard of any "Sessery" down in Clack, and nobody lived up on the mountain except Stig and Gom.

Gom's eyes widened. "Sessery's a *she*, not a *he*. She's Wind's second cousin. She lives down in the limestone caverns back of the mountain. I don't suppose you've ever been in them. She told me—"

He got no further. There they were, off again, hooting and rolling around until they were all gasping for breath. Mocking him.

"Gom Gom, dumb as a log;
His head's all wind, and his tongue's all frog!"

Gom waited, sighing. Serve him right for forgetting how different he was from them. Worst of all, it hadn't gotten Leadbelly anywhere.

Gom had nothing left now to offer Horvin—nothing

that Horvin would take, unless—Gom glanced at the jar. Leadbelly was jumping frantically up and down, banging his head against the lid. The mud was drying out, and the heat inside the glass must be suffocating. There was one more thing: his other new find. It was not nearly as valuable or interesting as the leaf or the bug in the stone, but maybe Horvin would think differently. Gom opened his pouch, took out the gold flake. He held it up between thumb and forefinger, turning it about to catch the sun. "How about this?"

"Oh!" the children cried. "Lovely! Lovely!"

"Where did you get that!" Horvin grabbed, but Gom swung his arm away and stepped back out of reach. "Deal?" he said.

"Deal." Horvin's eyes were locked on the flake.

"Promise?"

"Promise."

"All right," said Gom. He held out the flake, but still out of reach. "What when I win?"

Horvin grinned. "*If* you win—*if*—you win, you get the flake back, and all this other stuff here. When you lose, I keep it, of course, and the contest is over. Agreed?"

Horvin moved to take the tiny shining thing, but Gom stepped back again, closing his hand about it. "Not quite. When I win, I get the frog, too. Or there's no contest. Right?"

Horvin looked around at the children and winked again. "I'll think about it."

"For how long?"

"Tell you before the third jump. Now come on, Gom. Give." Horvin held out his hand.

Gom opened his fist, let the flake fall. Like a golden beetle shard it looked, lying in Horvin's palm. Horvin pocketed it.

"Cheat! Cheat!" the children cried. "It goes down there with the rest of the stuff until the game's done. You said!"

"All right, all right! It makes no difference," Horvin muttered. "I'll win anyway."

Gom winced as his brother pulled out the flake again and dropped it onto the pile of cracked marbles, half chewed jerky, stale oatcake, and lucky rabbits' feet. There was a bright flash, then the treasure slid out of sight among the rubbish. But it didn't break.

Horvin picked up the frog jar and held it on high. "Let the grand contest begin," he cried, and led the way to the back of the house.

CHAPTER ELEVEN

HE TRENCH WAS DOWN at the bottom of the yard by the compost heap. It was deep and narrow and slickery with water. Along its floor and up its sides, prickly twigs marked the various spots old Leadbelly was supposed to have jumped to, and hadn't.

"Here we are." Horvin lifted the top off the jar and dumped the frog out into the trench. Leadbelly flipped and flapped helplessly up its side as if trying to escape. Tilly squealed and grabbed Horvin's arm, but the frog only slithered back again and again gathering mud all the time. *Glung-a-lunga-liggerlug,* went Gom. *Glinger-linger-linger.*

Leadbelly blinked. *Glugger.*

("Fail the first two tries. On the third, leap clear and keep them busy until I call you. Agreed?")

("Agreed.")

Horvin crouched. "Ready, Gom?"

"Ready."

"Then set your stick."

Gom shook his head. "No need. He'll jump clear."

"Don't be daft," Horvin said. "I've been jumping frogs for eight years now and not even the best champ has reached more than halfway up—and this one's no champ!"

The children were laughing again, jostling each other, craning their heads over the trench side for a good view of the frog cowering in the mud.

"That's still my bet," Gom said.

"Hurry up, Horvin," Dugan said.

Horvin nodded, and with a stick prodded the tiny thing into place.

"One, two, three—*jump!*" he cried, and jabbed Leadbelly's rump.

The frog took off, hit the trench side blindly about a quarter of the way up, and flopped back again.

Glunger went Gom. ("That fooled them. Couldn't have done better myself.")

The frog made no sound.

All around Gom, the townschildren jumped up and down, clapping their hands and chanting, "One down and two to go; that old frog won't win, oh no!"

Horvin poked Leadbelly back to the starting point and counted again.

"One, two, three—JUMP!"

This time Leadbelly flipped feebly only to roll onto his back.

Gom frowned. Fake it, he'd told the frog. That was no fake. He leaned down into the trench. *Glugger-lug! Ligger-glung!* ("Are you all right?")

The frog didn't move.

Glinger-lung! ("Leadbelly! Answer me!")

There was no response.

Gom straightened up, met Horvin's triumphant smile.

"Ready for your *last* try, Gobblechuck?"

"I suppose so," he said. Then went on doggedly, "Do I get the frog?"

"Oh, I reckon." Horvin winked again at the others. "Yes, I reckon, don't you gang?"

"Don't do it, Horvin!" Dugan warned him.

"Yes, Horvin! Tilly says yes!" Tilly jumped up and down, flapping her hands. "Don't listen to Dugan. He always spoils the fun!"

"It's a trick," Dugan shouted. "You'll see."

"Rot, Dugan," Horvin said. "It clears the trench and it's home and free. Agreed, everyone?"

"Agreed!" the children cried.

Come on, Leadbelly, urged Gom. *Come on!*

All eyes were on the frog now as Horvin leaned over and for the final time shouted, "One, two, three . . . JUMP!"

At once Leadbelly shot clear up and out onto Tilly's blue-and-white checked apron, sprang thence onto Horvin's yellow thatch, then, leaping down, hopped about wetly under the children's feet.

"Catch it! Catch it!" yelled Horvin.

Mud was everywhere: on clean pinafores, cotton shirts, and pants and skirts, as the children either scrambled to catch or get out of the way of the slidey, slippery, bouncing frog.

Gom was shaken, too, but not for long. The clever little thing! Leadbelly had been faking after all—and so well that he'd even hoodwinked Gom himself! In the fuss, Gom ran around to the front, quickly retrieved the gold flake and restored it to his pouch. Then, taking off his jacket, he gathered up Horvin's treasure trove in it and made off. (Not that he really had any use for it, but he didn't see why Horvin should keep it.)

Down the street a little way, he uttered a loud croak whereupon old Leadbelly vaulted away, out and up onto his favorite perch on Gom's shoulder.

"You fool!" shouted Dugan. "I told you he'd trick you!"

Gom ran on. Horvin had thought himself onto a good thing: a frantic frog that jumped anyplace but the right one. It had brought what Horvin would consider a fortune in goodies.

"Hey! Gom! Stop! Come back here! You cheated!"

"Cheated? How?" Gom called back—without slowing up.

"Heard you—talking. Planned—it between—you! That's trickery, and it's not—allowed!" Horvin sounded quite breathless now.

"Planned it? Talking? Whoever heard of anyone talking to a frog?"

Glug! added Leadbelly, and through the blackness of his mud overcoat he puffed out a bright yellow throat pouch.

Gom reached the street corner. "Goodbye, Horvin," he shouted.

"Oh no you don't!" Horvin speeded up.

"Sit tight, Leadbelly," Gom said. "I'm going to have to lead them a dance or we'll never make it to The Wild Green Man."

Gom dodged away in between fences and hedges and by the time Horvin and company turned the corner, he was out of sight.

"Split up!" came Horvin's cry. "Don't let him go!"

"Talking of trickery," Gom panted as he ran on. "You certainly had me fooled, Leadbelly. I really thought you were a goner, you know."

"Good." The little frog blinked complacently. "For it made things more convincing, don't you think?"

* * *

By the time Horvin arrived, Gom had stowed Leadbelly safely in the horse trough at the back of the inn and was sitting beside Stig chewing away on a cheese sandwich as though he'd been there with his father all the time.

"Why, look, Gom. If it isn't your brother, Horvin, come to see us. How nice." The big man jumped up and hugged him, and what else could Horvin do but stand and submit?

"Horvin—" Gom reached down into his jacket bundle and pulled out the empty frog jar. "For you!"

"Eh," Stig said. "It fair does my heart good to see such brotherliness. Take it, Horvin."

Horvin took it. "You wait till next week," he hissed, grinding his fist into the tip of his nose, but Gom, his mouth full of bread and cheese, only shrugged. Next week was a whole world away. . . .

Munching steadily, Gom turned his attention to the old men sitting with his father on the alehouse bench. All they did was perch out there, day after day in the sun, gossiping. What a life, he told himself. What a dull, dull life, living in a place where there were no surprises, where nothing ever happened. He took a fresh bite of bread and cheese. He couldn't think how they ever—

A sudden loud croaking came from the back of the inn.

A call for help.

Leadbelly!

Gom sat up straight. Had Horvin guessed where he'd put the frog? Had he crept back through the inn's rear yard to recapture him?

Gom leapt up and ran around the building to find? Well! Gom stopped short. What would you expect to find by a horse trough but—a horse!

And what a horse!

It was short, and thick, and muscular. One hoof was black-fringed, the second was brown. The third was gray and the fourth, white. And its motley coat looked as though it had been pieced together with leftovers from other horses', reminding Gom vaguely of the patchwork quilts that the thrifty townswomen stitched endlessly.

As Gom approached, its red and brown and white and black and gray hindquarters were toward him and its head was down in the trough.

Glong-ung-lug! Leadbelly called. ("Help! He's swallowing me alive!")

Gom rushed forward and, seizing a yard broom, whacked the horse on the rump with its handle. That did the trick!

The horse's head came up smartly and at once Leadbelly leapt out of the trough. As he landed atop the pump, the horse lashed out with its hind feet and lifted Gom clear across the yard.

"Hey!" Gom scrambled up painfully off the cobblestones. "Just who do you think you are, kicking people like that? And what do you think you were doing with old Leadbelly?"

The horse looked him up and down.

"I am Pinosquat, pack horse to Dismas Skeller, Esquire. As for kicking you—what were you doing with that broom handle, may I ask?" It snickered. "Didn't anyone ever tell you how dangerous it is to cross a horse's rear? And as for what I was doing with that—creature up there—" It shot old Leadbelly a contemptuous glance. "I was *trying* to take a peaceful drink of water when it swam straight in between my teeth. Ugh. How would you like a frog in *your* cup?"

"He lies!" Old Leadbelly puffed out his throat. "He chased me around that trough until I didn't know up from down! And he'd have swallowed me alive if you hadn't come!"

Gom rubbed his backside where he'd landed on the cobblestones, and stared at the horse. Its accent was strange, almost unintelligible; nothing like the speech he'd learned from the horses in the town. Where had it come from? And who was "Dismas Skeller, Esquire"?

Would Stig know?

"Come on, Leadbelly." Gom turned to go, and as he turned, the horse neighing, lashed out again.

"Aha! I don't make the same mistake twice!" Gom cried, and dodging out of range of the horse's hooves, he added, chanting in his own, human, tongue:

> One two three,
> Fiddle-dee-dee;
> Bust your knee
> But you won't catch me!

"But I will!" came a soft voice behind him, and before Gom could say bread-and-cheese, he was seized from behind and hoisted into the air.

CHAPTER TWELVE

ITH A QUICK CROAK, Lead-belly leapt under the trough.

Gom, his legs pedaling wildly, tried to turn his head.

The hand shook him by the scruff of his neck, then, still gripping his collar tight, set him down and spun him around.

Gom found himself looking up at the biggest man he'd ever seen—except for Pinkle, the blacksmith—and Stig, of course.

But he was a different kind of big; not muscle and brawn but *bony* big, with a scarecrow's broomstick shoulders, long arms and long straight legs like potters' chimneys.

And the rest of him!

On his great bony skull was set a wide red hat trimmed with green feathers that blew briskly in the wind. From his large ears dangled great thick rings that shone bright yellow in the sunlight, reminding Gom at once of the flake tucked away in his pouch. The man's smock was of purple velvet, faded and worn, while his breeches, much patched, to be sure, were striped in yellow and black.

The man pulled Gom close and bent down and down until they were eye to eye. He smelled of stale spice and tobacco smoke and his eyes were black as Gom's own, only hard, very hard. Gom's knees went weak. "Father," he called, but the word stuck in his throat.

"What," said the man, "were you doing in my packs?" The voice was still soft, unexpectedly soft for such a big raw fellow, and the accent short and clipped with a whispery hiss.

What had he been doing with what? He noticed then that the horse was carrying two packs on either side of its roly-poly body, and that the flap of one of them was hanging loose. Surely the man didn't think that he, Gom, had opened it! Gom stared up into the man's eyes, unable to speak.

"Cat got your tongue?" The man's wide thin mouth turned up. A cruel mouth. "I'll try again. What's your name, little man?"

Gom swallowed.

"G—Gom. Gobblechuck. Gom G—Gobblechuck."

The man's hand tightened on Gom's collar until Gom began to choke.

"*Gobblechuck?* What kind of name is that? Say whose house you're in, and why I've not seen you before. Quick, before I slit your scrawny little throat."

"Gom?" Stig's voice came from the corner of the inn. Quick as a fox the stranger loosened his grip on Gom's collar, moving his hand as though extending to Gom a friendly pat on the shoulder.

"Speak one word about our little chat, Gom Gobble-chuck, and you're dead meat—remember that!" The man let his arm fall, releasing Gom.

Gom backed out of reach, still looking into the man's eyes. How his shoulder hurt. But he dared not rub it. Such a violent threat the man had uttered, and for no good reason that Gom could see. Who was he? Where was he from? And what was he doing in Clack?

"Oh—Gom—there you are. I wondered where you'd run off to." Stig beamed at the stranger, seeing him take his arm from around Gom's shoulder. "Why, hello again, Sir Dismas," he said. "I'm right proud to present my son. I'll bet he sensed your horse back here. That's why you ran off, isn't it?" He turned to Gom again. "Gom, this is Dismas Skeller, Esquire, Royal Purveyor from Far Away, that came by the town six days since with wonderful things to trade and tell."

Gom moved round to stand by Stig.

"Royal Purveyor?" He looked the man up and down, feeling braver now from the shelter of his father's arm. "What does that mean?"

"It means, my little man," Skeller said, "that I go from place to place trading the Queen's good wares in return for whatever homely articles her subjects may have to offer. 'Tis a service Her Majesty appointed me to perform for the benefit of poor folk like you."

Queen? Her Majesty? Gom had never heard of one. Neither had Stig, Gom was sure, nor anyone in Clack. "Who's that?"

"Why, the Queen of Far Away is the most important person in all the world," Skeller said. "She's very very rich, and she lives a long long way from here in a large castle with many many soldiers who fight many many wars on your behalf. So you should be grateful to her indeed, and for the things she sent me to sell and exchange with you, as I've already told your father, and all the rest of the townsfolk here." He smiled briefly, putting Gom in mind of Snake's lipless mouth opening to swallow one of Lead-belly's young. "They say your father here makes very fine carvings, and indeed, from what I've seen, Her Majesty would think right well of him for supplying me with a hundred of them or so."

"But as I've told Sir Dismas," Stig said hastily, "I've never made that many at one time, and I've never any left by this time of the year."

"*And* he tells me that he, quote, 'doesn't have time to make me any either.' Her Majesty will be most disappointed. Oh well, it's time for me to make my rounds." He turned to Stig. "Good day."

"But," Stig said, in his anxious-to-please voice, much to Gom's dismay, "I would buy you a jug of ale if you're disposed to sit awhile. Your tales of Far Away are powerful interesting."

Skeller, who'd already moved off, came back at the mention of the ale. "I'd be most honored," he said.

Gom walked on ahead with Stig around to the inn front, feeling strangely uncomfortable with the man at his back. So sinister, he was. Threatening. And worrisome, too.

Most of what Stig earned came in food and staples. What little money he got was from the sale of winter carvings and from odd summer jobs like carting, mending fences, building rock walls, and such. To think his father was not only pleased to sit with such a man, but he was about to squander that hard-earned money on ale for him . . . and yet—what was all that about Far Away?

In spite of himself, Gom sat down to listen to what

the stranger had to say, taking care that Stig sat between them.

Far Away. It did sound exciting. But scary. A body could get lost *Far Away*, Gom was sure, for hadn't he seen that bodies going far away grew smaller and smaller until they disappeared?

It came to Gom then that his mother also had come from Far Away, and had returned there after he was born. Maybe that man had heard of her—had met her even, perhaps? He glanced at his father's face. Was Stig wondering the same thing? Was that why he wanted to hear about Far Away? Gom clasped his hands together between his knees, longing to touch the rune, to feel its comforting vibration, but could not. Not before company, and certainly not in front of that strange man.

He listened intently as Stig plied Skeller with ale again and again. At last, however, despite his interest, Gom grew restless, then alarmed. Their small earnings for the week were almost gone. And for all his long-winded tales, the man was saying very little at all. Just enough to keep the ale flowing, always coming to an interesting bit—about cities of gray stone, and lands locked in ice the year round, and dark forests full of rare timber—just as his mug ran dry so that Stig would fill it up again—and everybody else's—to keep him talking.

The gaffers, Gom noticed, didn't shuffle off as they usually did for their afternoon snooze, but sat, thanks to Stig's easygoing generosity, getting a free ear- and bellyful. How he resented them, especially old Gaffer Gudgeon, the miser. He was far better off than Stig, and yet here he was drinking up Stig's hard-earned money and never even offering to buy a round in return.

What could Gom do? Well, maybe he could change the

subject, perhaps, and satisfy his curiosity at the same time. "Those are strange rings you have through your ears," he remarked, as Stig brought out yet another jug of ale. "What're they made of?"

Skeller looked at him sharply. "Why, they're made of *gold*, little man," he said. "A rare and precious metal you'll not find in many places."

Oh really, thought Gom, fingering his pouch.

"*Gold*. 'Tis a goodly name. We have golden things hereabouts, and though they might not be of that stuff exactly, they're still very fine. Show Sir Dismas your golden loder leaf, Gom," Stig said with pride.

Reluctantly, Gom produced his wooden box and raised the lid.

"Humph," Skeller said after the briefest glance. "Very nice, I'm sure. It would look quite fine on Her Majesty's bodice *if* it were *real* gold. So many trinkets she has made of it, as everyone knows, for gold is her favorite metal."

"Has she earrings like those?" asked Stig, picking up Skeller's mug for a refill. "Powerful handsome that gold looks on a body, I do declare," he went on. So busy he was, staring at the earrings, not watching what he was doing, that the mug overflowed and the ale ran down its side, onto Skeller's velvet smock. "Especially in the ears. There's nothing like it in Clack."

Gom looked at his father in surprise, noting the look of frank admiration on his homely face. He tried to picture the earrings dangling on either side of his father's cheeks, and couldn't. And yet—it was plain that Stig was much taken with them.

"That's not surprising," Sir Dismas said, taking back his mug. He frowned at the froth still dripping onto the shabby velvet of his smock. "As I've already said, 'tis a rare metal indeed. The Queen herself gave me these earrings when she made me a Sir."

"A Sir?" Gom had heard of a Master, for was not he addressed as one when folk were minded to be polite and amiable to him? And a Maister, for that was what they called his father, and Bok, and Pinkle, and Craw. Mistress he knew—Hilsa's title now that she was married—and Gaffer—he looked around at the old men sitting about—and, just now, Queen. But a Sir?

" 'Tis a title that Her Majesty gives those who do her good deeds. You kneel on a cushion and the Queen taps your shoulders with a sword. It's a great moment. Then she says, 'Arise, Sir Whoever,' and there you are."

Gom was fascinated. "What does that signify?"

"Signify?" Skeller frowned. "Why, it signifies that I am more powerful and important than you'll ever be, that's what, little man."

The gaffers cackled, old Gudgeon the loudest.

"Anyway," Skeller went on, ignoring Gom now and addressing the company in general, " 'Arise, Sir Dismas,' the Queen said, 'and accept these gold earrings as a token of my appreciation for all your good work around the countryside among the poor and needy.' She's promised me a chain thick as your arm when I'm done with this pack load."

Gom persisted. "If I wanted them, what would you ask for them?"

Skeller's laugh was surprisingly harsh. "Why, more than you could ever earn. Gold, my little man, is the coign of royalty."

Gom stared at the light winking on those earrings with the movement of Skeller's head, his temper rising. Much as he feared Skeller, he didn't like being called "my little man," and being made to look small in front of old fogies who looked down on him enough already—especially Gaffer Gudgeon. He'd show Skeller, he would. He'd show them all. His father wanted earrings? Then he'd have them, dozens and dozens of pairs, bigger and better than those in Skeller's ears. Gom would show them all, every last one of them. He'd make these people sit up and take notice of him at last. "That's lucky," he cried. "For I won't need them. We'll get our gold elsewhere."

Old Gaffer Gudgeon began to wheeze like Maister Sproggins's bagpipes. "Don't mind him," he said. "He's a cocky one. Master Know-it-all, we call him—no offense, Maister Stig," the old man added hastily. He turned his watery eye on Gom. "You don't find gold same as iron and copper and silver. It's rare. So rare that them earrings is all even this Royal Purrywayer has. You'll not find it around here." He cackled. "So stuff your mouth with bread and cheese and keep it shut."

That did it. "Not find a piece around here?" Gom said, opening up his pouch. "Really? Then what about—this?"

Lifting the pouch flap, he shook his small treasures into his open palm: seeds, the pod of a hoarbell, a honeybee's pollen sac, a moon moth's cocoon . . . and . . . that tiny fleck that flashed in the glare of the sun.

That same flash caught Skeller's flat black eyes, and Gom's triumph turned to fear. Too late he saw that far from being clever, he'd just made the biggest mistake of his life!

CHAPTER THIRTEEN

ELL! I NEVER!" Gaffer Gudgeon cried.

Stig's large blue eyes grew very round. "Shakes and shingles," he said, and rubbed his head.

Skeller leaned over Stig and held out his hand. "Allow me," he said, and what could Gom do but comply?

Skeller took the tiny gold flake, turned it over in his palm with a long thick finger, and scraped it with his thick yellowed thumbnail. Then he laid it on the tip of his tongue.

Gom winced. His lovely bright shining flake of sunshine ruined! Now the man looked set to eat it! If only Gom had said how soft it was, this might not have happened.

"Umm," Skeller said at last, and spat it out. " 'Tis low grade ore. Too base to be of use. Here."

Gingerly, Gom took it back again and returned it to his pouch. It shines as bright as your earrings, he wanted to say, but dared not. What, he thought, if something else besides the gold's shine determined its value—say, its hardness? Hadn't he shown his ignorance enough for one day?

Skeller got up from the bench, stretched and yawned.

"Well, 'tis past time for my rounds," he said. "I move on in a day or two, and I must do right by the Queen." He nodded farewell to the gaffers. To Stig he said, "I hear you come down the mountain but once a week. I likely shall be gone when you return. Pity. The Queen shall take it ill that Clack's woodcutter bought nothing from her stores."

Stig's face went very red. "I'm but a simple poor man," he said.

"Not too simple and poor to spend an afternoon outside The Wild Green Man shouting ale for one and all," Skeller said with a grim smile. "Good day to you, Stig."

No "Maister." No "thank you."

And in two strides he was gone.

Gom had never felt so angry in his whole life: with his father, with Skeller, with the old gaffers, and most of all, with himself for being such a fool.

He glared down at his empty plate.

Not fair! Not fair! he said inside himself over and over again. That man had not only walked away with all their hard-earned money in his belly, but he'd had the gall to insult and threaten Stig into the bargain! And Gom was helpless to get even or put matters right. He was glad that the man would be gone by the following week. Good riddance to him! Gom wouldn't care if they never saw a Royal Purveyor again!

"Well," his father said at last, with his keeping-a-cheerful-face-on-things smile. "At least it's a nice day."

Old man Gudgeon scowled up at the clear blue sky. "That's what you think. My knees tells a different tale."

"Oh?" Stig's smile faltered. It was a common assumption in the town that the older a body got, the more he or she knew about the weather, so much so that folk would take the advice of the gaffers even if it were wrong more often than right. So Gaffer's warning of a storm was bad news to Stig. "Oh dear," he said. "I was so sure it was going to be fine, I didn't bring a cover for the cart and our week's food will be ruined. Oh, whatever are we going to do?" He ruffled up his hair. "Maybe if we leave right away we'll get home in time."

Gaffer shook his head. "Sorry to dash your hopes, but I said to myself first thing, I said, this sky's a fool's sky, but it don't fool me. Could hardly get out of bed with my knees, and that allus tells me the weather's going bad."

Gom watched Stig's face getting sadder and sadder. As if his father hadn't been treated badly enough that day already. First that butcher, Bok, trying to cheat him out of his fair due; then Horvin, looking like the dutiful son when he'd really been after Gom; then Dismas Skeller, scrounging Stig's hard-earned money from him by telling false tales—helped by these sponging old gaffers, too. And now this miser, Gudgeon, was upsetting him with claptrap about the weather! He jumped to his feet. "Your knees told you false," he cried. "There'll be no rain today, nor tomorrow, nor for another week or more, just as my father said. He knows more about weather than any of you ever will."

Gaffer's knuckles tightened on his walking stick, and for a moment he looked set to use it. "Oh? Well, I repeat, *Master Know-it-all* that you'll not get home without a dousing. I'll lay a week's bread and ale on it!" For emphasis, Gudgeon looked around at his cronies, his mouth working, his head going slowly up and down on his scrawny neck like a turtle's.

"Done!" Gom cried, so triumphant over certain victory that his anger evaporated instantly. "That'll save us a deal of money, won't it, Father? You are including the cheese, too?"

"Why, the impudent puppy!" Gaffer shouted, half-rising on his bench. He fell back, coughing, and picked up his empty beer mug, affected to drink from it, then tipped it up, looking pointedly at Stig.

Stig opened his mouth.

Why, he's going to offer to buy him another, Gom thought in a panic. "I'll tell you how I know," Gom said quickly.

"Oh, you will, will you? What do you know of rain?"

"I know," Gom said, "that Wind's been yonder"—he pointed up over the mountain peak—"to visit his sister, Zephyr. It's so warm there, he told me, and so dry, that he's always in good spirits for a week or more after coming home. You'll see."

Gaffer looked around. "You hear that? The lad's gone quite dotty at last. Comes oi running wild up there instead of living down here like other folk—no offense, Maister Stig, but it's not good for him."

Stig stood up miserably. "Gom, we ought to be—"

Gom also stood, beside his father. "Wrong again, Maister Gudgeon. And as for your knees—"

He broke off in surprise. His head was beginning to buzz again. And for the second time in two days! He stood there, watching bright pictures pass across his inner vision, a smile spreading over his face. When they were gone, he paused for a moment, clinging to Stig's arm until the dizziness passed, then opening his eyes again he fixed them intently on the old man's face. "The ale's all right for you, but not the stuff you take when you go to bed. *That's* what makes your knees bad, not rain."

So saying, Gom bent down, picked up his jacketful of

trophies and dumped them into the cart among the meat bones, the dripping, the sausages, the bartered honey cakes, the cheese, the potatoes, and young green beans.

"Here, here, you young rascal," Gudgeon called after him. "Not so fast. What do you mean—'the stuff I take when I go to bed'? Speak plain!"

"I mean the plum brandy, Gaffer. At least, that's what the pictures say on the label. There's a bunch of plums and the sign that means bran—"

"Plums? Plum brandy?" Gaffer raised his stick and waved it about. "Get that lad out of here before my hand forgets itself and takes to his backside! Plum brandy, indeed! Why, everyone here knows what I think of folks who drink that sort of stuff!"

"But I saw you drink it. As plain as I see you now."

"Saw me—" The old man turned on Stig. "You mean to say that you let that boy out in the middle of the night to come snooping down here, peering—" He stopped, but too late, much to Gom's delight. Why, the old hypocrite had quite given himself away!

"No, Gaffer." Gom tapped his skull. "I saw you in here, just now when I closed my eyes. You had a blue nightcap on, and a red-and-yellow nightgown with a green-flowered patch on the elbow."

"Get him away! Get him away!" Gaffer hopped up and down brandishing his stick. "Lad's not only brash and unmannered but a liar, too!"

"Eh, come Gaffer," Stig said soberly. "My son is a good boy." He took Gom's arm and drew him toward the cart. "Come on, lad. It's time we went home."

But Gom was not yet done. Fair was fair, and Gaffer owed Stig. "Does the bet stand, then?" Gom called to the old man.

Gaffer looked around at his cronies then back to Gom. Gom only just managed not to smile. Gaffer was trapped, and they both knew it.

" 'Course it does, and right sorry you'll be afore you've taken many steps, mark my words."

Gom let his father lead him then, stopping by the trough for old Leadbelly. He began to whistle softly, thinking of how that old miser was going to have to shout them lunch for seven straight town days on end, and that was for the rest of the summer, and all the way through into the fall.

* * *

Leadbelly rode Gom's shoulder until they were well clear of the town. As they went along, the old tree frog told Gom of how two nights before he'd followed a huge swarm of midges down the mountain into the town. Of how he'd eaten so many he'd fallen asleep under a water butt. Of how the next morning, he'd woken up trapped inside Horvin's jar. "I should have had more sense, I see that now," he croaked. "Tadpoles and tiddlers, you'd have thought that at my age I'd learned not to follow my nose like a young green thing without taking my wits along!"

Gom nodded, remembering uncomfortably his own adventures of the day before.

"However," the frog went on, "I've certainly learned my lesson this time. Never again will I leave the creek—unless it's with you, of course," he added. "Twice you saved my life today. I thank you most heartily, and until our next meeting, goodbye." So saying, he sprang down from Gom's shoulder to take his own route back up the mountain, eager and hungry to refill his empty belly on the way.

Stig and Gom tramped on up the steep trail.

But they hadn't gone far when it dawned on Gom that Stig was unusually quiet. In vain Gom waited for Stig to strike up a song. At last he was forced to ask, "Why aren't we singing this evening, Father? As you always say, the way seems so much easier with a tune or two to help us along."

Stig stopped the cart.

"Since you ask me, son, I'll tell you: I have one or two things to say to you, and I don't rightly know how."

"Well," said Gom, "how about the beginning? That's always a good place to start."

"Easier said than done," Stig replied, ruffling up his hair. "Look: Gaffer called you a liar. And while I said him nay, while I'd uphold your word against another's any day, I can't help but wonder—you said you saw him in his nightgown drinking plum brandy. But if you didn't go down into town to spy through folks's windows—how *did* you know about the brandy and what he was wearing when he went to bed?"

Was *that* all? Gom felt relieved. "That's easy to answer," he said. He tapped his forehead. "I saw him in here when I closed my eyes, just as I said."

Stig stared at him, shaking his head, and looking strangely disturbed.

"You don't believe me, Father?"

"I do, I do, and I'll tell you what I've never told no man. That's what your mother, the Wife used to do. Fair shook the wits out of me, she did, at times. And here you are, your mother's true son. Has it happened before?"

Gom nodded, feeling gratified. "Oh, yes." He almost told his father then about his dream of the day before, when he'd found the gold under the mountain wall. But on second thoughts, he decided not. So he said instead, "Remember last month when you couldn't find any decent oil-wood and I said, 'Let's try down by the Dip,' and we found those four old trees just lying there? Well, I saw them, just as clearly as I saw Gaffer Gudgeon just now in his nightcap. It doesn't happen very often, and rarely when I want it to, but happen it does."

Stig regarded him in wonder. "Why didn't you tell me about it?"

Gom looked surprised. "I never thought. I mean, why should I? I didn't know it was so out of the way."

Just as it had never occurred to him until lately, until the townschildren began to mock him for it, that talking to Leadbelly and Snake and Sessery and Wind were anything out of the way, either.

. . . *your mother's true son* . . . Absently, his hand sought the rune.

And as Gom stood there on the track looking up into his father's simple face, he became acutely aware of how different he himself was from other folk, and it made him feel peculiar; a little excited, a little frightened, and not a little superior to the townsfolk down below—even, a little, right then, to Stig.

But there was Stig, still looking down on him solemnly, still with something left unspoken. "There is more, Father?"

"Oh, I don't know, my lad." Stig reached out and ruffled up Gom's hair. "It's just that—I'm a mite anxious over your tongue. Brash, Gaffer called you, as well as a liar, and while I know what a good boy you are at heart, and honest, and willing to help anyone, yet it seems to me that you do strike folk that way.

"Son: quick and clever is your mind, and marvelous strange. And for that I'm right proud of you. But too quick, and too clever it is at times, and lacking in proper thought for others. They say pride goes before a fall, and I'm not minded to see you suffer one.

"Take today: you were rude to the butcher, for a start."

"He cheats you, Father, and steals from you. I can't stand to see it."

Stig nodded. "Yes, well. But time and again I've told you that I don't mind. Then you were a mite hasty and loud with the Royal Purveyor—an important man the Queen says we must respect. Why did you have to brag about the gold?"

Gom hung his head. *From pride and an itch to score over Gudgeon and Skeller* didn't sound too impressive. He looked up again. "Skeller's a fraud and a cheat. I bet he's never seen any Queen. He says all those things only to make folk buy his wares. Don't trust him, Father. He's an evil man. You know who he reminds me of? Bobcat on the prowl. Be glad we've seen the back of him."

And as Gom said that, he was doubly glad, remembering the look in Skeller's eyes on seeing the gold flake flashing in the light of the sun, remembering the look the purveyor had given him in the rear courtyard, and the words he'd hissed in his ear, *Speak one word about our little chat . . . and you're dead meat—remember that!*

How lucky that the gold wasn't so valuable as he'd thought—and Skeller must have spoken truly there, for hadn't the man suddenly lost all interest in them, even in Stig's free ale?

Oh, what a relief it was to be on his way out of it all. No more having to watch out for Stig being cheated. No more threats from angry grown-ups like Bok and Gaffer Gudgeon. No more feuding with Horvin, or mockery from the rest of the children, or feeling the outcast. And right now he was especially glad to have left Skeller behind.

He thought gratefully of Sessery, of Wind. Of Leadbelly, of Blue Jay—even sour old Hoot Owl. Up here he was welcome, and at home. Up here he was on familiar territory that held no bad surprises, and safe among friends.

Perhaps—yes, and perhaps that Skeller wasn't so right about the gold after all. Perhaps tomorrow Gom would go to harvest more of it and see if Pinkle couldn't make his father a pair of earrings like Skeller's—nay, better!

He realized that his father was still waiting, expecting some kind of answer to his words. "I'm that sorry, Father," he said, "if I've caused you trouble. For your sake from now on I'll try extra hard to mind my manners and curb my tongue. *Now* may we have a song?"

Stig picked up the shafts with a relieved smile.

"Aye, lad. We'll have a new one today, about a young apprentice called Lollybob, whose prideful tongue so ran away with him that the people chased him clear out of town until he'd mended his ways. It'll have a lot of verses, enough to take us all the way home. You can join in the chorus each time it comes, beginning, *O woe is me, for I am run out of town.*

> There was a lad by name of Lollybob,
> A fine upstanding lad was he;
> Who went to town to find himself a job
> A 'prenticeship to candlemakers three.

"Now, Gom," Stig said. "Listen to the chorus and sing it with me after the next verse. It goes:

> O woe is me, for I am run out of town,
> Run out of town, run out of town;
> O woe is me, for I am run out of town,
> For letting my tongue run free!"

Gom listened, then waited while his father sang the second verse:

> He kissed his mother and he walked away.
> "Farewell, my lovely son," she sighed;
> "Remember this and that and every day
> To keep a bridle on your foolish pride."

"Now you, Gom," Stig prompted him. " 'Tis time for the chorus again."

"O woe is me," Gom chanted happily above Stig's rich brown voice, once and twice, and the rest of the way home, and as he fell asleep that night, for all the good the words had done him, he was still humming the tune.

CHAPTER FOURTEEN

A T BREAKFAST THE next morning, his father announced that he was going to cut big timber by Woodchuck's Hole, that he could manage quite well by himself, and that Gom could take the morning to be about his own affairs.

"Noontime I'll meet you here for a bite or two and then you can help me split and stack. Suit you fine, son?"

Gom nodded over his tea mug.

Times before Stig had gone off on his own for a while. And this was during the rare times when Stig was sad. All through the night his father had tossed and turned on his creaky cot, sighing and groaning. And Gom was sure it was for the Wife. That Skeller, with his stories of Far Away! He set down his mug and without a word put his arm around his father's wide shoulder.

Gom resolved to go back to the gully to fetch out some of the gold to cheer his father up. Maybe—maybe if he brought out enough they could swap it down in Clack for the many things they'd always needed: fresh linen sheets; a big bottle of rubbing oil from Mother Chubb, the herb woman, for Stig's back when it was bad; hard cheese that improved with age no matter how hot the weather; a whole *barrel* of ale for Stig; a warm jacket for his father with a high collar to keep his neck warm on cold mornings. And new boots—for them both! Yes, fetching up that gold would do a deal of good!

Out they went as the sun hit the rooftop, Stig upward, Gom down; each waving the other out of sight with a "See you at elevenses," and "Take care."

Gom strode along, whistling the Lollybob song. He wondered whether to ask Leadbelly to go with him, and decided not. That one had probably had quite enough of traveling for a while!

He reached the blasted pine to find it empty. He was just about to climb down into the gully when he heard the jingle of a bell. He looked this way and that, listening.

Wings fluttered suddenly overhead, nearly toppling him down the gully. The mocking bird was back. "You've a tall, tall, tall, tall shadow," it called. "A tall, tall . . . tall . . ." He flew off again.

Gom turned. And grinned. The early sun, slanting across the mountainside, had stretched his short shape way behind him to blend in with the shadows of the trees. "Get you for that!" he called.

Again he heard the bell, back through the trees, along the way he'd come. Now he recognized it: the mocking-bird's latest addition to his repertoire—a cow bell. Not the deep low kind, but a small tinkling one, a lighter one that the farmers used down below for cows grown old.

Chuckling in appreciation, he began the downward climb.

It wasn't very pleasant in the gully so early in the

morning. The night mists still lay about its rocky ground, and everything dripped with icy dew. It would be hours before the sun struck through, too late to do him any good. He walked upstream as he'd done before, and stood at the pool's edge, huddling into his jacket.

He looked down. The water was cold and dark. Opaque. No sign of gold flakes today. He looked up. He couldn't see above halfway up either bank.

Yesterday morning at this very hour he was in the town, with the new sun already striking polished windows, heating the street cobbles, sending fresh fragrances from the neat, bright gardens with their neat, bright flowers, setting up air currents for the gnats to ride—a world away from this dank gully bottom that stank of wet lichen and moss.

He moved on under the deeper gloom of the mountain wall. And as he walked, he heard again, way up overhead, the jingle of the bell. That mockingbird is doing himself proud this morning, Gom thought. He's singing fit to make one bell sound like a full plough harness!

Gom wiggled through the rock slit and stood beside the stream, his boots barely visible in the dim light that drifted in with the mist. But that didn't matter. This time he didn't need light.

After only one trip he knew this tunnel well enough to travel "blind," as Sessery had taught him to: feeling direction by her drafts on his cheeks, judging a roof height from her echoes, the firmness of ground by the vibrations under his bare feet.

Bare feet.

He took off his boots and socks, stuffed the socks into the toes of the boots, and left them by the slit. Then he sidled along the narrow ledge between wall and water, his palms flat to the rock, his ears alert, until he reached the little cavern.

There, he paused, listening to the water flowing into it from the farther hole, then grunted in disappointment. If he'd really come through Sessery's secret back door, as he suspected, he'd gotten no farther than her rear hallway. To go any deeper under the mountain, he suspected, he would have to go through that inner hole. And there was no way he could pass through that, for he could tell by the water's gushy echoes that it was a drowned tunnel. What a pity, to find a door that he could never use.

Still, Gom wasn't sure how useful the back door would be. He'd already decided that he was below the level of the limestone caverns because of the glistening dark rock of which this back hall was made. And because of the stream. Gom knew the limestone caverns thoroughly, and he'd never come across one. No, this stream ran below them, below any level that he had ever gone. And he'd never ever found the way down to it. So perhaps there wasn't one.

So even if he did get through the drowned tunnel— where could it lead him? Nowhere that he wanted to go, probably. In any case, he had no idea how long the tunnel was, whether it was crooked or straight, whether it went up or down, or whether he could get through it, and he certainly wasn't going to try to find out, for that way a body could drown!

With a sigh Gom turned away from the drowned tunnel to the shallow pool in which lay scattered the small knobs of yellow metal like so many golden eggs. He took off his jacket and spread it out beside the pool. Then rolling up his breeches, he waded in and cast about him for the gold.

* * *

When at last he was ready to leave the cavern for the warmer air outside, his teeth clicked together with the cold and his feet were numb.

He rolled up the nuggets in his jacket and tied the sleeves together around it so that the nuggets wouldn't spill. Then he made his way back along the outer tunnel and crawled through the low rock slit, pushing the gold out ahead of him, out into the daylight.

He was no more than halfway when he was startled by the jingle of bells close by his ear. That pesky mocking-bird again! Didn't he know when a joke was stale? He certainly needed a word or two of adv—. Gom stopped in mid-thought. In plain sight ahead of him stood four hooves: one black-fringed, one brown, one gray, and the other, white. Pinosquat, full packs bulging out from his barrel sides, was by the basin drinking, and as he drank, the bells on his scarlet harness jingled musically.

How in the world, thought Gom, did that animal get down that bank, and loaded like that? He never did have the time to find an answer, for a moment later a hand gripped his collar, dragged him out into the open, and hoisted him high into the air.

CHAPTER FIFTEEN

O, MY LITTLE MAN. We meet again. Isn't that nice?" Dismas Skeller set Gom down, keeping tight hold on his collar. "Keep quite still, Gom Gobblechuck. You and I have business," he warned, as with his free hand, he reached for Gom's jacket.

Gom watched the man's face as he untied the sleeves and opened it out, tumbling the gold onto the rocky floor. That same look of utter greed was back in the glint of the eyes, the tightness of the mouth. He noticed now how like a beak Skeller's nose was: the vicious, hooked beak of a hawk. It came to Gom then that the man had killed, not once, but many times, and would again if it suited him, without a second thought.

Skeller looked up. "That's good, very good, my little man. Don't you think, Pinosquat?"

Pinosquat looked up and snorted, jingling the bells

again—a hollow sound in that hushed, lonely place.

Gom looked around vainly for help. For a blue jay, or even that mockingbird, who, he now realized, far from teasing him, had been trying to warn him. *You've a tall, tall, tall, tall shadow . . .*

That shadow had been Skeller. And ironically, the bells had not been the mockingbird's call but real bells, the bells of Pinosquat's harness. How stupid the mockingbird must think him not to have realized. And what a fool Skeller thought him already not to have bothered muffling them.

Gom remembered now the bird's answer two days before when Gom had asked him where Leadbelly was. *Down, down, down, down,* he'd told Gom. Gom had thought he'd meant that Leadbelly had gone down into the gully, when obviously the bird must have meant the town. That mockingbird had tried to help him twice, and twice Gom had not twigged it. How stupid he'd been!

Gom opened his mouth to shout for help, caught Skeller's eye and closed it again.

Laughing, Skeller produced a short pointed knife, which he waved before Gom's face. "Very wise. Very wise indeed. Now: you are going to be my worker, little man. Tell me—how much more of this lovely gold is back through there?" Skeller put the edge of the blade to Gom's throat. "Speak the truth," he added, or it will go the worse for you."

Gom looked back at him bravely. "How can anyone know that in the dark?"

Skeller shook him. "That's not the way to speak to a Sir. How far in is it?"

"Not—too far."

"Umm. And this is the only entrance, so you'll not be sneaking out on me—oh, don't look surprised. It's not so hard to guess. There can't be any other way, or you'd have used it and not played the mountain goat down here. Now: you're going back in, again and again until you've brought out every last speck of gold. And if you've not filled this bag by noon . . ." Skeller put the knife back at Gom's throat.

Gom swallowed hard. "If you don't let me go in a minute," he made himself say, "you'll have to do your own work. You're choking me."

Skeller laughed again, and setting the knife back up his sleeve, he let go his hold of Gom's collar. "There now. Now you're quite free—to turn yourself right around and get back in there. Go on, hurry up. You've work to do—for the Queen."

"I'll bet!" Gom stood up straight and faced Skeller angrily. "There isn't any Queen, is there? And you're no Sir. You're a liar and a swindler, who cheats simple folk out of their good things with worthless trash!"

Skeller only laughed the louder, and reaching into a bundle by his feet, he brought out a tinder box and a knobbly torch-brand, which Gom recognized with a start as coming from the side of the hut. Why, the man must have been by the night before, watching through the window as he and Stig sat by the fire taking their supper—maybe still spying on them as they'd lain asleep. Gom shuddered. The hut door was never locked.

It occurred to Gom then that the man must be leery of Stig's great might and size, even when his father was asleep. For the first time in his life Gom felt Stig's absence. Knew what it was to be without him. In that moment, Gom felt really and truly alone.

Skeller coughed. "Pray, do take your time, little man. Don't let me disturb you. But remember: I meant what I said about filling this bag by noon."

Gom looked at the bag in despair. "I'll never fill that if I try for one hundred years," he said. "There's not that much gold in there."

Skeller hauled him close and stared into his eyes. Then he pushed him away again. "Then see that you bring every last piece out," he said. "After that you can dive for the pretties." He pointed to the flakes swirling about in the rock pool.

Dive?

Gom wasn't going to *dive.* Not for anything. Not even for Skeller. His spirits rallied. "That would take too long," he said. "I'll fish them out with my jacket. Clean the pool out in no time."

"Your jacket?" Skeller said thoughtfully. "All right, we'll see about that when you've finished in there. Now—move!"

Gom got onto his belly and wriggled through.

Noon couldn't be so far off. Almost time for elevenses. His hopes rose. Maybe he could play for time, and when he didn't turn up, his father would come looking for him. But here? His hopes sank again. Stig hadn't asked yet where he'd found the gold flake, and Gom certainly hadn't said.

"Here!" Skeller called from the other side, and pushed the torch-brand and tinder box after him.

"Don't need it," Gom called, and ignoring Skeller's reply, he stood up and tried to think.

So he had been right about the gold being worth something. Of course, Skeller's loss of interest had been but a trick. The man must have followed him home, and from there, down the gully. He thought again of the man standing out in the dark, spying on them through the hut window, biding his time until he could get Gom alone;

following Gom all the way down here. He shivered in the cold. What a *fool* he had been!

Now Skeller had him trapped into fetching out the gold. And after that?

The Royal Purveyor certainly wasn't going to pat him on the head for all his trouble. He could just see him now: "Well, thank you very much, little man. Give my regards to Stig and tell him the ale's on me the next time I'm by. . . ."

No. That one wouldn't leave him alive after he'd fetched out the gold, not if there was a chance of more. He'd surely want to keep the secret to himself.

"Are you still there, Gobblechuck? Hurry. I haven't all day!"

Gom stayed where he was.

Of course, he could do just that.

Stay there until the man gave up and went away.

But could he? Skeller would never give up. Well—neither would Gom. He'd *starve* before giving in, see if he wouldn't!

"Hey!" Skeller's voice grew harsh. "Haven't you gone yet? I see I'll have to teach you a lesson, little man."

Gom heard a splash. Skeller was coming in after him, diving under the stream! He moved then, all right, almost tumbling into the stream in his haste.

He emerged into the cavern space and squatted at the far edge of the pool. Skeller was coming after him. In a few moments, he'd be there, at the entrance to the cavern. What then? There was only the one way out, not counting the drowned tunnel, which he certainly wasn't going to take.

He pictured himself trying to sneak back out of the cave past Skeller; Skeller seizing him again and hoisting him into the air. Skeller drawing his knife and putting it to his throat. A faint light wavered on the wall around the tunnel bend.

Skeller? Of course! Carrying the torch Gom had so obligingly left for him! What a double fool he was this day!

"Gobblechuck?" The soft voice came nearer. "Where are you, Gobblechuck?"

The light erupted into the cavern, reeking of sweet resin and smoke. Skeller, hatless, and bent double under the low roof, came out into the cavern and straightened up, blocking the entrance completely, a giant in that small space. He raised the flaming torch the cavern's full height, and his shadow twisted back behind him, writhing on the glistening walls.

"So there it is—and there you are. Well, well, well. I shan't need you now, you know. So first—little man—I shall with great pleasure snap your scrawny neck. And then I shall take out the gold myself!" he cried, and made for Gom.

CHAPTER SIXTEEN

HE BIG MAN came at him. Gom
bent down and smacked the wa-
ter hard with the flat of both hands, making a big loud
splash. Startled, Skeller dropped the torch.

Flame hit water with a hiss and all went dark.

"You'll pay for that, little man," Skeller called softly.

Gom stood up and held quite still, waiting for the man's
next move.

Skeller's voice came again out of the darkness. "I know.
You want me to come after you, don't you? So that you
can sneak past me in the dark. Well, your plan won't work,
for Dismas Skeller is too smart."

Gom heard him wading back to where the tunnel hit
the cave.

"Come on, little man!" Skeller's voice cracked the
hollow space between them. "I'm ready for you. You just
try to sneak by and I'll slit your gizzard!"

Gom didn't move.

Neither did Skeller.

Water plop-plopped into the pool.

From behind Gom the little stream rushed breathlessly out from its drowned tunnel, past the shallow pool, past the Royal Purveyor, and on along the outer tunnel to daylight and freedom.

"This water's not overly comfortable, is it, little man?" There was an edge to Skeller's voice now. "My feet are numb, and these are my best boots that you've ruined. I'm afraid that if you don't give yourself up very soon, instead of slitting your gizzard, I'll have to pick you apart piece by piece."

Gom bit his lip. The choice wasn't exactly improving. What could he do? There was only the one way out, and Skeller was blocking it. Unless—No. To take the drowned tunnel was unthinkable. He'd already decided that.

Nevertheless, he waded cautiously across the shallow pool and wincing, stepped down into the stream, and began to pull himself against the current toward the back wall where the waters burst out into freedom. The flow was strong, and deep, and deadly cold.

He cried out suddenly as a spout of water, hitting him full in the chest, nearly swept him back into the pool. He went still, listening. Had Skeller heard? Did the man guess where he was going? If so, Gom realized he must hurry. Gasping with the cold force of the flood, he struggled on until roof arched down to meet floor. At his feet was the low round hole from which the invisible waters gushed.

Into that tunnel he must go. It was the only way out.

He thought of the water rushing up his nose, filling his mouth and throat, and lungs. He pictured himself stuck in that dark closed space: drowning; too weak to go on, with no room to turn about and come out again.

He was shivering violently now, from cold and from fear. He thought of Stig up above in the warm sunlight. How grieved his father would be, when Gom didn't come home. *Oh, Father.* His hand closed about the rune.

All at once, there came a violent splashing and Skeller's voice came again. "So: you make me come for you after all. You'll pay for this. Little man, you go too far!"

But not far enough, thought Gom. As Skeller bounced and splashed his way toward him. Gom took a deep breath—then plunged.

* * *

There was a roaring in his ears, and great pressure.

For a long time—how long?—he clawed his way along the tunnel against the tearing current. It was narrow, barely wide enough to take his shoulders. Was he making any headway? It didn't feel like it. How much longer? He began to count, trying not to panic, wondering how far he'd get before his breath gave out. One, two, three, four, five—hand over hand—sixteen, seventeen, eighteen. His chest started to hurt, and lights flashed behind his eyes. He kept going until—forty-eight, forty-nine—his lungs gave out at last.

He pushed upward, expecting to smash his head against the tunnel roof, but instead he bounced up into cold rushy air filled with Sessery's light laughter.

So he sneaks in the back way today like a water rat, instead of calling on me properly, through my front door.

Gom lay face down on hard rock beside the stream, unable to speak. Then after a moment, he coughed, rolled over and breathed deep. "Sessery? Help me! If I can go from here up to the limestone caverns show me how, please. It's urgent!"

Sessery chose not to answer him.

Gom sat up. "Sessery! This is no time for games! I'm going for my life!"

Still no reply. Trust Sessery to play hide and seek just when he needed her. Hadn't she told him often enough how she was above trivial human troubles? This Gom could well see and understand, but yet he'd always thought of her as a friend. It hurt him to think that she cared for him no more than he would, say, for an aphid fleeing mantis jaws.

Gom hauled himself painfully to his feet. Only this morning he'd thought how good it was to be back home safe on the mountain. Now everything was changed. Into his own backyard had come the worst evil, to lay violent hand on him and to threaten his very life!

Father, he thought. I must find Father. He must go. But where? How was he going to find the way—if any—out of there? "Bother you, Sessery," he called. "I don't need you. I'll find my own way."

And who . . . taught . . . you . . . how . . . eh? her mocking whisper came.

"Sessery?" The tease! She'd been there all the time.

You're no fun at all, she complained. *Where's your sense of humor today? Silly. You're not lost. How can you be lost under one small mountain? Come: stretch your hands and toes before you, just as you always do. . . .*

He obeyed, feeling Sessery's gentle currents on his skin. A few steps and he had the floor incline. A few more, the direction. He kept going straight until he sensed a shaft of the hard, sharp bedrock directly above his head. "Does this lead up to the limestone level, Sessery?"

Maybe—and maybe not. You'll have to see, won't you, small one? Sessery spiraled up and up the shaft and out of reach.

Gom, sighing, climbed after her.

Up, up, he went, up the vertical shaft wall. It seemed to go on and on. Gom went with the greatest care. One careless move and he would slip without hope of breaking his fall.

All at once his head began to spin. Oh, no! Not one of his waking dreams now! He would surely lose control and let go! He clung desperately to the sheer rock face, while flecks of light came and went in the darkness and all at once he was aware of the rune vibrating, prickling his chest, almost painfully, as before.

Gom had the feeling suddenly that he was no longer in the narrow shaft, that he was in another space, even though he could still feel his fingers and toes clinging to solid rock. Through that rock, some way ahead of him, as from the end of a long, long tunnel, there appeared a dim light, a lovely warm and amber glow, shedding its radiance on low, arched walls.

A cavern.

The light brightened, dazzling Gom's eyes, until at its center shone a skull. Gom stared at it fixedly, feeling an irresistible pull toward it; to tread that tunnel to the light.

His real surroundings forgotten, Gom made to move forward, only to press his body up against solid rock. The rock of the vertical shaft.

He came to his senses abruptly.

The glow faded, and the skull. The rune ceased its vibrating, leaving Gom only too aware of the peril he was in; of dark space beneath him, of his precarious hold on crevices and cracks.

He shook his mind clear and resumed his climb. But the vision of the skull remained. What had it meant? Was the skull calling him? And if so, why? And where was it?

If it was really under the mountain, it lay in a place that Gom had never found.

Was he meant to seek it? he asked himself again. And the rune: was it urging him on, or warning him away? It was certainly trying to tell him something.

No time to think about it anymore, for he was suddenly out onto level ground once again. Ground that felt softer, smoother, and more familiar.

Why, he was at the bottom of the main limestone tunnel, at the far side of the mountain. To think! The times he'd gone down there and never once noticed that narrow shaft connecting the limestone layer to the dark and secret roots of the mountain. He strongly suspected that Sessery hadn't meant him to.

"Thanks, Sessery!" he called, then moved on, along the tunnel, turning, twisting, going up and up and round along a path he knew well.

On he went, faster, until he came to a fork, where another passage came from the right to join the main one, making it wider, and higher. Another turn and he was in a vast space filled with stalactites and stalagmites, treacherous spikes springing from roof and floor, like a cougar's fangs grown wild. That space he crossed, never putting a foot wrong in the darkness, even in his haste, picking up the tunnel again at the other side. Now Gom had no idea how long he'd been under the mountain, but he was sure Stig was missing him by this time.

He went on a little farther then slowed, despite his haste, for a little way in front of him was a deep crevasse, a split across the tunnel floor narrow enough to take at a leap but wide enough to fall down if he didn't mind his step.

Some way beyond the crevasse the tunnel suddenly

ended in a wide space where five tunnels converged. Sessery's front hallway at last!

Gom emerged into twilight. Good gracious, he thought. His father would be frantic! He ran on and on through the trees, and across the clearing toward the hut. The door was open wide.

"Father!" he yelled, but no answer came.

The table was set for supper. The bread was dry, the cheese sweaty, and the ale was warm and flat.

"Father! Father!" Gom ran out again, shouting.

Unmindful of the cold, his bare feet, the wet clothes still clinging to his body, of whether Skeller was on his trail, Gom headed out into the forest calling his father's name over and over at the top of his voice.

OOoo called Hoot Owl from his hollow tree. "What a carry on there is in this neighborhood today, and no mistake! First that great father of yours goes crashing past here yelling 'Gom!' at the top of his voice, starting me from my hole. And now you, just when I was recovering myself. It's a conspiracy!" Hoot Owl puffed out his feathers, then preened them down. "Your father sounded very upset. What have you done this time?"

"Where," Gom cried up at him, panting, "did he go?"

"I know," a sleepy dove murmured from a neighboring tree. "Woke us up from our siesta, he did. Now here you are rousting us out all over again."

Gom stopped under the great oak in which the dove's family was roosting. "When! And where did he go?"

"Why, way before sunset. And quite a bit before firefly time. Running all over he was, then he took off that way." The dove pointed a wing. "Talking away to himself a fair sparrow, too. Such a quiet neighborhood this is but today we might as well be sitting in the middle of town!"

Gom stared stricken along the way the dove had pointed.

"To the *limestone caverns*? But why?"

"I heard him say," the dove told him, "that since he'd not found you anywhere else, he was of a mind to seek you there."

CHAPTER SEVENTEEN

TIG in the caverns! Worse and worse!

He ran back the way he'd come.

His father didn't know his way about that place at all. One wrong move, one clumsy step and he was surely dead.

Racing on, Gom remembered Skeller. Was he still waiting down in the gold cavern? Surely not. More likely the man was coming after him back up from the gully and round, for he'd never fit through the drowned tunnel. In which case—Gom looked about him as he ran.

Something to his right caught his eye, a glimpse of glowing colors in the darkening forest: red, and purple, and yellow and black—Skeller, with his hat back on, running down toward him. Skeller, racing to head him off.

"Stop!" Skeller cried. "Stop! I'm not going to hurt you! You must help bring out the gold!"

Gom speeded up. Help bring out the gold, indeed! The

man was out to kill him. Zigzagging among the trees the way he'd learned from the rabbits, Gom sprinted the last few hundred yards into the dark of Sessery's front hall.

Behind him heavy steps crashed closer through the undergrowth. Skeller's long legs were gaining fast.

Lose him, Gom told himself. Lose him, before you go any farther. You can't run around calling "Father!" with Skeller about, for you'll only tell him where you are.

He paused, looking at the five tunnels leading from the hallway. Which one had his father taken? As he stood trying to decide, bats squeaked by on their way out for the evening. Had they "seen" Stig? No, they told him. Not Stig nor anyone.

The hungry bats flew past him and away.

Which direction should he take? Gom assessed his options. Of the five tunnels, two belonged to the bats. According to them, Stig had not gone down either of those. Which left the other three.

Just outside Sessery's front door, he heard a sudden angry yelling, and a loud twittering, high-pitched. Skeller had met the bats.

Gom must move. But which way? Quick, he must decide.

"Sessery? I'm looking for my father. Where is he?"

In a pretty pickle, that's for sure. Clumsy creature that he is, that has already come to grief and will come to worse, if he doesn't hold still. Here, follow me, and I'll take you to him.

To Gom's surprise, Sessery wafted him into the tunnel leading up from her back door.

"But I've only just come up from there, Sessery. Father wasn't there then."

So? He is now. Come.

Gom set off, following Sessery, the soles of his bare feet scarce touching the cold rock floor. Ahead was the crevasse. Gom felt a surge of panic. Surely his father hadn't fallen down there! "How far along here is my father, Sessery? As far as the crevasse? Is he still all right?" he whispered.

Perhaps, Sessery whispered. *And perhaps not. He's lying like a stone. On.*

Gom's panic increased. His father *had* fallen down the crevasse. How far? "Father! Father!" His voice echoed off the tunnel walls.

From behind him, there came a shout. "Gobblechuck—come back, I say! You'll have to give up in the end!"

Skeller! Gom ran on grimly. The man was still following him! Had somehow taken the right tunnel. Gom began to suspect that the Royal Purveyor had trodden mountain mazes before!

Gom slowed for the crevasse.

On, little one. He's not down there.

"Then why didn't you say so in the first place!" Gom cried angrily. He leapt the narrow space, and ran on.

Only to stop again. What if Skeller fell down there? It would be Gom's fault. He, Gom, would be responsible for the death of a man. . . .

He waited, uncertain, until he heard a shout.

"Ah! Hoped you were rid of me, I bet, Gobblechuck. But it's Dismas Skeller you're dealing with, not—"

Gom lost the rest of it among the echoes preceding him into the hall of stalactites and stalagmites. ". . . n-o-o-t . . . n-o-o-o-t . . . o-o-o-t . . . o-o-o-o-o-o-t . . . o-o-o-o-o-o-o-o-t . . ." The man had leapt the crevasse and was coming on!

The last echoes of Skeller's shouts all but overwhelmed another distant sound coming faintly from beyond.

"Help . . ."

His father!

Gom sped into the tunnel beyond, and down until he came to the fork. There, he halted, listening to the sound of his own breath. The cavern behind him was silent, and silent was the space ahead. He'd lost Skeller at last! "Father! Father!" he called, at the top of his voice.

"Gom? Boy—is that you?" Stig's answer came faintly up the left-hand passage, the one leading down to the deep shaft.

"Father! Father!" Gom shouted, and ran toward the sound.

But not for long. Careless in his eagerness, he neglected to use his ear for judging echo, and his face for catching Sessery's quick warning drafts. Suddenly, his feet encountered empty space where none should be, and he fell headlong down.

CHAPTER EIGHTEEN

E DIDN'T FALL FAR.

He crashed onto something firm, yet a little soft: his father's chest. "Father!" He teetered, snatched Stig's arm and held on, righting himself. They were on a narrow ledge partway down the rock face.

"Father!"

"Where *have* you been, son?"

Before Gom could answer him, Skeller's voice came from overhead.

"Gobblechuck? You're not so smart as you thought you were and—I hear another—that wouldn't be your father, would it? Dear, dear. Not hurt, I hope?"

Before Gom could warn him, Stig spoke up. "Is that Sir Dismas Skeller? Thank the skies! Whatever brings you down here? I'd thought you gone to Far Away today."

Gom tugged Stig's arm. "Father—"

"Hush, my son." Stig patting Gom's hand, gently disengaged himself, then put his arm around Gom protectively. "Sir Dismas? My son and I are in a pretty pickle here."

"Stuck, are you?"

"Yes, sir," Stig called back up. "Will you help us?"

"Father," Gom said.

"Help you? Oh, yes," Skeller said. "I'll help you."

There was a scraping, grinding sound and a fair-sized lump of rock whizzed past them, striking their ledge and bouncing on down.

"But I don't—" Stig sounded bewildered.

"He's helping us, all right, Father—to our deaths. He wants the gold."

"Gold?"

There was no time to explain. Another rock came tumbling down, and another. Gom reached up, pulled Stig's face down to his level. "Father," he whispered in his ear, "whatever I do, hush, and keep quite still." He pressed Stig against the rock wall.

When the next boulder came by them, Gom screamed, loud and long, tailing off at the end—a pretty fair rendition of a gray goose flying over the mountaintop, Gom thought. To his great relief, Stig kept his peace. Now perhaps Skeller would think they'd fallen to their deaths and go away.

"Gobblechuck?" There was a silence. The silence lengthened. Skeller wasn't yet convinced. Oh well, they could all play the waiting game. Now: when Skeller had gone, Gom was going to have to get his father up off that ledge. In the dark. Which wasn't going to be easy. Oh, how much longer was that man going to hang about? Suddenly, Gom felt a tickle up his nose.

Aaaa—aaaa—He was going to sneeze! But he couldn't afford to. He breathed deep through his nose and out through

his mouth, quietly. It only made it worse. *Aaaa—aaaa—*
In a panic, he pinched the top of his nose, just where it
bent, hard, between his thumb and forefinger. There.
That was better. The tickle was quite gone. He lowered his
hand again, and there it came ripping out of him:
"*Aaaaach*-oooo!"

Skeller laughed. "Gobblechuck? Good try, little man.
But not good enough." The man scrambled down, knock-
ing Gom sideways. A strong hand groped, found and seized
Gom's shoulder. And it wasn't Stig's. He felt Skeller's free
arm shake once, with a short, snapping motion. He remembered down in the gully, Skeller's producing a knife
seemingly out of thin air, his waving it in front of Gom's
face; his sliding it back up his sleeve.

"Father!" Gom called. "Skeller has a knife!"

Gom had no very clear idea of what happened after that,
only that he heard an awful angry *growling* sound, like that
of a bear roused too early from its winter sleep. Why,
that wasn't Skeller—it was his father! Stig, who'd never in
all Gom's life raised his hand even to a mosquito, was
wrestling with a killer.

Gom pressed himself up against the rock wall and
covered his face. The ledge beneath them trembled. It was
cracking under the strain, Gom could tell. At any moment
it would give way. Then they'd all perish. There was a
smack as the two great bodies hit the rock face, a thud as
they rebounded off it.

"Father!"

There came a loud rumble, then a cry, a full long roaring cry, that thinned away, down, and down . . . and down.

Then there was silence.

"Father?" Gom whispered.

There was no sound.

For long he stood there, not daring to move, then fearfully he reached up to touch . . . a shoulder? Yes, a shoulder, a big shoulder—not bony big like a broomstick scarecrow, but a firm rounded shoulder, all muscle and brawn.

"Father! Oh, Father!"

Gom put his arms about Stig's middle and squeezed tight.

Stig stirred. "Sir Dismas—?"

"Gone."

"Gone?" Stig whispered.

Gom nodded in the pitch dark. "Yes. *Really* gone. Are you all right, Father?"

"I—think so, son."

"Good," Gom said. "For the rest of this ledge is going. We must climb."

"*Climb!*"

"Yes," Gom said. And added briskly, "So take off your boots."

"My boots? For why, son?"

"The better to feel your way up the crevices, Father. Quick!"

Without another word, Stig took off his boots, tied the laces, and hung them about his neck.

"Father—keep still!"

Stig cried out as more of the ledge gave way.

"Here, Father. Give me your hand." Gom found a crevice and guided Stig's hand to it. "Here, Father, put your hand here." He found another for Stig's left foot, then his right. Half a minute more, and Stig was clinging rigidly to the wall with Gom beside him. They'd made but one more move when with a rumble the entire ledge beneath them gave way altogether in a rush of dust and grit.

Gom was overcome by a helpless fit of sneezing and coughing.

"There!" cried Stig. "This is what you get for hanging about this place in the dark and the cold! The times I've told you about coming down here!"

Gom had a foolish urge to laugh. There was Stig, hanging onto a perilous rock-face, his only perch gone from under him, scolding Gom as if they were back at home by the hearth!

A sudden scraping sound brought him to his senses.

"Son, my foothold's given way! I'm slipping."

"Steady, Father!" Gom said. He reached over for Stig's dangling foot, guided it to another crevice. That crumbled, and Stig lost both footholds, hanging on now only by his fingers. Quickly Gom found him fresh ones, more solid this time, and in another minute they were both lying up on the tunnel floor well away from the cave-in.

Gom's head felt hot and sticky. He raised his hand to his face.

That wasn't sweat; it was blood. And not his blood but his father's.

"Father, you're hurt!"

" 'Tis but a scratch. That Skeller's knife. I'll live. Glad I am to be out of that place, and grateful to you for getting me out. You're a good boy."

Gom hung his head in shame. Stig would never have been in there in the first place had he not come looking for his son!

"But how," Stig went on, "are we ever going to find our way out? I know I was wandering for hours and hours before I fell down there."

"Why, I'll take us out easy, you'll see."

Gom led his father away, back up the passages, over

the chasm, through the stalagmite cavern and up, up out under the stars.

"Why," said Stig as they came out. "You went about that place just as though it were bright as day. I'd never have believed it if I hadn't witnessed it with my own eyes."

Gom began to laugh.

"What's the jest, son?"

"*With my own eyes*, ho-ho-ho, ho-ho. Don't you see? You said you'd *witnessed* me down there—in the pitch-dark—with your own eyes!"

Stig stared at him for a moment, then he began to laugh, too, until the nightwood rang with the sound.

Stig stopped suddenly. "That Dismas Skeller. That were a bad do, and no mistake. A bad do."

Gom nodded soberly. "And it was all my fault."

"Eh, no son." Stig laid his hand on Gom's arm. "You had no choice in what happened."

"He was after that gold, Father."

"Aye. So you said."

"Then that gold is evil."

"No, son. The evil was in the heart that craved it. The desire for riches does bad things to people. Even desire for ever so little. That's why, son, I never mind about it. Life's too short to be twisting up your chest over it. Good luck to them that has it, I say. As for me, I got my treasure right . . . here!" And with that, Stig scooped Gom up, threw him over his shoulder, and strode toward home.

They hadn't gone above half a dozen steps when Gom was taken by a fit of sneezes, one after the other, as if he would never stop.

"Just hark at you!" Stig quickened his steps. "Bed for you, son. You've gone and given yourself a right chill and no mistake! And where are your boots!"

Gom saw them quite clearly where he'd left them just inside the rock slit. He sneezed again to change the subject. Time tomorrow to talk about boots. Truly tired by now, Gom closed his eyes and bumped along, hearing Hoot Owl's cry over his head, something about Gom's looking much better that way up.

He was too exhausted to think of a reply.

CHAPTER NINETEEN

N THE EARLY HOURS, Gom awoke, sweating. The hut was stifling. Embers burned in the hearth. And he was lying not only under his own comforter, but Stig's.

His father was deeply asleep.

Gom's throat was sore, and his whole body ached—but that was too bad, he thought, for he had something to do, and before daylight, before his father could stop him. He slipped out of bed and looked around for his boots, then remembered that they were back down the gully. His jacket, too. Quickly, he slipped on a jacket of Stig's that reached down to his knees, and crept barefoot from the hut into the chilly night.

*   *   *

"Son! Son, wake up!"

Gom opened his eyes, wincing at the light.

"How do you feel?"

Stig was bending over him, a mug of hot tea in his hand.

"Fine, Father, fine."

Gom sat up, took the mug.

Stig sat on the bed and felt Gom's forehead. "You've a fever."

"No, Father. I'm hot because the hut's hot. I'm fine, really I am. Father . . ."

"Yes, son?"

Gom stared down at the tea-leaf floating on top of his cup, round and round, like the great red hat he'd seen floating in the rock basin in the moonlight. "Father, if I tell you something, promise not to be angry."

Stig looked puzzled. "For sure, why should I ever be angry at you?"

Gom set down his mug and reaching under his bed pulled out his wet, rolled-up jacket. "For you." It fell open and at once a cascade of gold lumps spilled over the cover and onto the floor, shining dully in the early morning light. "There's more, *much* more, Father, where that came from, only I couldn't bring it all up by myself."

"You mean—" Stig look incredulous. "You went out again *last night*?"

Gom nodded. "The whole point of yesterday was to get you that gold. Now we can take it down into town—not to sell it for money," he added hastily, seeing Stig's coming frown. "Rather we can exchange it for some comforts for ourselves."

"Well, I'll be . . ." Stig said. "To tell you the truth, I did wonder where your boots had come from." He nodded back toward Gom's boots steaming by the hearth. "I might have guessed." He turned his round blue eyes back on Gom. "You know, son," he sighed, "I think I should be angry at you for doing what you did, but a man might as well be angry at a squirrel, or a bee, or a 'possum for doing its own natural thing." He reached out and ruffled Gom's hair.

Gom closed his eyes in relief, and thought how lucky he was to have a father like Stig.

The bed sagged and creaked as Stig bent to pick up the gold pieces that had spilled out onto the floor. "There's more, you say."

Gom opened his eyes. "Aye, Father. Lots and lots. And gold flakes in the basin—only I—thought I'd leave them until today." Again, he saw the broad hat with the limp feathers whirling round and round like a monstrous lily pad. What a shock it had been to see it. Gom had almost taken to his heels back up the gully side. "The lumps are all piled ready by the mountain wall. Six times I had to go back under the rock slit, Father. We'll need the cart. I would have used Skeller's packhorse, but it's taken off somehow. So may we go back now, Father, before we start work? I'd like to get all the gold out for us and have done with it, so we never have to go down into that place again."

Stig's frown deepened. "I don't rightly know, son. I'm not going to work today, in any case. I already reckoned as how I ought to go back down into town to tell what happened yesterday. A man shouldn't suffer his passing without comment, you know. Not even Sir Dismas. It's not right."

"Then you certainly should fetch the rest of the gold now, Father. We can take it down with us and trade it today. Say yes. Please."

Stig laid his hand again on Gom's brow, and shook his head. "You feel mainly hot to me."

"It's the fire, Father, and these comforters. I kept them on, see?"

Stig smiled his slow smile. "Aye, I see. And I daresay you took the fire and your bed and those comforters down with you to fetch out the gold. All right, son. I'll go down into that accursed place. But not so much for the gold as to see if I can't see sign of that poor man."

"You won't, Father. He's gone too deep. So we might as well take the cart, and a log bag, and—oh—my other shirt to fish the pool for flakes. The townsfolk will all be wanting it so badly, there won't be enough to go around. Oh, let's hurry with our breakfast, Father, and be on our way. You'll not regret it, you'll see!"

*   *   *

They left the cart by the blasted pine and climbed down, Stig slipping and sliding heavily most of the way.

What a remarkable animal was that patchwork quilt of a horse, Gom told himself, losing his balance and taking a painful slide on his rear end, to get down that bank all in one piece—and up and out again!

When they reached the gully floor, Gom led his father upstream to the basin.

"Why, isn't that Sir Dismas's hat?" Stig pointed.

Gom nodded, looking despite himself. The wretched thing, snagged now on a jutting rock, bobbed up and down with the current. It made him feel quite queasy to see it, even in daylight.

Leaning over, Stig peered down into the bottomless

depths of the rock basin. Gom followed suit, fighting an unpleasant tightening in his gut at the thought of what he might find, but he saw only the hat and the gold flakes forever roiling about. He straightened up and drew Stig on upstream to the rock slit.

There, scattered in front of it, lay a great pile of gold pieces.

"My my, son. That must have took hard work." Stig unslung a canvas log carrier from over his shoulder and spread it on the ground beside the pile.

"Yes," Gom said. "Actually, I truly didn't mean to bring all that out, but once I got started, I couldn't seem to stop."

Gom moved forward and began to load the first lot of gold onto the canvas. Then, while Stig was carrying it up the gully side, he took up his other shirt that he'd brought with him and cast about in the basin for flakes. He didn't get them all, but enough. Not that he and Stig needed them. But it seemed only fitting to Gom to take them now, for after all, finding the flakes had been the start of the whole business.

After some hesitation, Gom also fished out the sodden hat with a long stick and buried it under a flat stone, without touching it.

Six trips it took Stig to haul that gold out of there and pile it onto the cart, but at last his father bundled up the stout log bag for the last time and climbed with Gom out of the gully—Gom with his jacket bulging with flakes, as many as he could carry.

By the time they reached home, the sun was well over the hut roof and Gom was sweating a fair lick.

Stig took one look at him and sent him back to bed. "I shall go alone today. And perhaps 'tis fitting that I do.

Death is no business for a young lad. You stay in bed, do you hear?"

"But," Gom protested, "I must come. I always come. You need me."

"Nonsense," Stig said, banking up the fire and setting more logs by the hearth. "How do you think I managed before you came along, eh? You stay there, son, and do what I say for once."

"Then at least wait to take the gold down," Gom said.

Stig shook his head. "The gold will buy you the cough syrup you need, and a warm vest to cover that chest of yours. And a new pair of boots." He glanced back to Gom's old scuffed and worn ones, now stiff and dry. "I'll do well, trust me."

"It's not you I don't trust," Gom said. "It's them."

But Stig went alone for all Gom's protestations, and took the gold with him.

Gom dozed the day away, getting out of bed only to drink the broth Stig had left for him in the hearth, then tottering back to lie against his pillows, thankful in the end, that his father was gone for the day, for a fever was indeed upon him, and such a sneezing and a coughing that his father would certainly have fussed over, had he stayed at home.

At last, Gom fell into a deep, deep sleep.

A slight rattle woke him, then the click of the door latch.

"Father?"

There was no reply.

The hut was dark. Gom lay on his back, unable to move. Was he awake? Or still asleep? He couldn't tell, so real was the room around him, and the sound of the latch.

The door creaked open.

Gom turned his head. Someone was standing there, just the other side. Get up, he told himself, but he couldn't, for a terrible numbness was upon him.

"Who—who's there?"

A movement in the hearth made him cry out.

A log had shifted, collapsed. An ember flared, a pocket of unburned wood ignited in a shower of sparks casting a wavery light on the hut walls. Gom looked from the flame back to the door.

He watched the sliver of red hat brim slide from behind the edge of the door. The sliver waxed like a sick moon until Skeller's face appeared. The face was smiling, the mouth tight and cruel.

"So," Skeller said softly. "We meet again. What a coincidence."

Gom tried to shout, to move, but all he could do was lie there and watch the man snap the gleaming knife from his sleeve and slowly walk toward him across the floor. *Father*, Gom called, but only in his mind.

Skeller, his clothes still wet, was standing over him now, his eyes dark sockets in the wavering firelight. "Too bad your plan didn't work, little man," he said, and raised the knife to strike.

CHAPTER TWENTY

G OM REMEMBERED imagining that blade between his ribs. He could feel the pain now, the sharp thrust of it. Oh, it hurt, it hurt, and he couldn't even cry out. . . .

"Gom? Gom? Hey, lad, wake up!"

He opened his eyes. The hut was filled with lamplight and the smell of burnt toast. Stig was shaking him gently by the shoulder. Of Skeller there was no sign. Gom became aware that he was lying, not flat on his back as he'd thought, but curled up on his side with his fist caught underneath him, pressing painfully into his ribs. He must have been having a nightmare after all.

"Son—son—feeling better?"

Gom sat up, rubbing his side. "Oh, much, Father. How did it go?"

"Well, there was a big fuss, and no mistake." Stig went to the hearth, put a slice of slightly charred toast onto a plate, poured a ladleful of steaming broth into Gom's mug, and carried them over to him. "They're all afraid that when the Queen hears about Skeller she'll send her soldiers to kill us all, but I said we've nothing to fear if we tell the truth. For what Skeller did wasn't right, not right at all. But in the end," he finished sadly, "they still seemed more afraid for themselves than angry at what he did to us."

Gom dunked his toast into the broth and took a good big bite. "You know what I think, Father?" he said, with his mouth full. "There isn't any Queen, and if there is, she doesn't know about any Skeller. I was right. That man was a fraud and a cheat—worse, a killer. Why should we believe a word he said? If the townsfolk want to fret for a while, that's their affair, not ours. But what about the gold? Did it trade well?"

Stig turned back to the hearth, picked up the toasting fork, spiked a thick slice of bread with it, and held it to the flames.

"Father—the gold—did it trade well?" Gom asked again, but he knew the answer before Stig got the words out.

"Son—I—well, I—" Stig stopped, then said in a rush, "I *gave* it away."

Gom's broth tipped over the bed. "You *what*?"

"They were that angry with you, I had to."

"Angry with *me*? Because of Skeller?"

"No, not exactly. To tell you the truth, it were strange. I told them all how clever you'd been, finding your way under the mountain and all. Boy's a regular wizard, I told them. But it only made them mad. They don't seem to like the idea of wizards, at all."

Gom was shocked. "A wizard!" His father couldn't have said a worse thing! "Oh, Father. They say down there that wizards are bad people who cross your eyes and blight your

crops; set fire to haystacks and sour the cream in the churn.
You've heard them say yourself that if ever one were to
show his face down there, they'd run him out of town."

Stig tried to laugh. "I'd like to see that, lad. I really
would! Surely froth on a beard makes a man brave! But they
know no better, and how should they, never having traveled, never having seen a magical man? What they say is
born of fear and ignorant superstition. Oh, there are bad
wizards, just like there's bad of everything in this world,
but for the most part, wizards are very wise people who
know much much more about things than us ordinary folk."

"Like what, Father?"

"Oh, everything. The whole world. What makes the sun
shine, what makes the rain. How to cure a gaffer's gout
better than Mother Chubb can, and how to stop Mistress
Merry's cough. He—or she—knows how to stop toothache,
and charm the wart off the end of your nose. How to make
dry wells run again, and temper spring floods. A wizard
knows all about signs and letters and numbers and books;
about the stars and the best times for planting, and how to
double your cow's milk.

Gom stared at Stig, fascinated, despite his consternation over the gold. "Father, how do you know all this?"

Stig's face sobered, grew wistful. He stared at Gom as
though not seeing him, then looked away to the hearth.

"Your mother told me," he said, at last. "Long, long
ago. She'd traveled the world over and over. Many things
she told me of a winter's evening, but"—he ruffled up his
hair—"it's all gone from my head, save what's come back
to me today about wizards."

Gom felt a prick of excitement. He took his mother's
rune from inside his nightshirt and looked at the lines and
squiggles running riot over it.

A wizard knows all about signs and letters and numbers and books. . . . Gom didn't know a single sign, neither did any of the townsfolk. They could all count after a fashion, it was true, and keep tally with rough notched sticks. Were these numbers and letters on this little black stone? he wondered, and as he wondered, he felt a faint vibration coming from deep within the stone. Scarce able to hide his excitement, he put it to his ear.

Nothing.

"What is it, son? What are you doing?"

"Listening, Father. Father—" He thought excitedly of his visions of the gold and the skull in its strange amber glow, of the way the rune had almost pained him, so alive it had been, lying against his chest. "Father, you know what I think? I think that these lines are letters and numbers. And if they are—was Mother—?" He faltered at the shocked expression on Stig's face, then pressed doggedly on. "Was— *is* she a wizard, do you think?"

Stig went a deep red, then to Gom's surprise, he laughed outright. "To tell you the truth, son, she might very well be. 'Twere strange, the way she popped up out of the blue, and disappeared again. And I allus said she wouldn't have left us without good reason. And wizards have good reason. For they have such important work about the world, you know. Why, they really do speak with queens, too. To think," he said, looking wistful, "that she bided full thirteen year with me."

Gom leaned forward, forgetting his broth, his toast, everything. His mother—a *wizard*. How wonderful if it were true! He was almost of a mind to tell his father about the visions and the rune there and then, but something, some inner caution stopped him. So he merely asked, "Can you tell me anything else about her? About them? Think, Father. Think hard."

Stig screwed up his great round face, and squeezed his blue eyes tight. "Well, it were marvelous the way she knew the leaves and roots and such. I never was ill all the time she were with me, nor were the children, not for long at any rate. And she allus seemed to make the food go around, somehow, though I don't know how. And I swear she spoke with the critters out in the woods the way you seem to, though it seems hardly possible to me. She certainly weren't no ordinary woman. That's why the townsfolk didn't take to her as they might have, though they were right kind to her, I will say that. But goodness knows what they might have done if there'd been a breath of a whisper about her being a wizard. I think we'd best not talk about it again, son, if you don't mind." The glow left Stig's face, leaving it sad again, which made Gom glad that he'd kept his peace.

"You mean—they think *me* a wizard? Just because of what you said?"

Stig nodded unhappily. "I was only trying to show them what a clever boy you were, telling how you'd saved me from Skeller and gotten me out from under the mountain, knowing your way about them caves and all. But it only made things worse. They said it weren't natural for a boy to know so much, and to get the better of grown men. So I gave them the gold."

But Gom *hadn't* gotten the better of Skeller! It had been the other way around! And there was nothing special about knowing Sessery's territory, for hadn't she taught him everything? But it would be useless to try to explain to the townsfolk. Once their minds were made up on anything, that was that. He looked at Stig's troubled face.

"But what of your earrings, Father? The whole point of bringing out the gold was so that you'd have some."

Right then, Gom thought ruefully, it appeared as though everybody and his uncle was going to have a pair but Stig.

"Oh, son. I'm that sorry, but after yesterday, I couldn't, don't you know?"

Gom knew. He sighed. It was no use being angry, for Stig was what he was. As for giving away the gold—he'd known that would happen, hadn't he? He was sure now that somehow his mother's rune had been trying to help them, to show them the gold to ease their poverty. But the plan had failed, and a man had died because of it. And after all that they were no better off than before. Oh, if only he'd gone down into town with Stig! But he hadn't, and that was that. Now all the gold was gone.

No—not quite all.

He thought of his jacket under his pillow, filled with some of the best nuggets and a veritable bucketful of flakes. He'd bury it as soon as he was up and about again, and save it for a rainy day. He smiled up at Stig. "So: they'll not run me out of town now, then, having the gold?"

Stig looked relieved. "Oh, no. The blacksmith's going to be working day and night to forge it into chains, and earrings. Why, some have so much that they're even going to have scissors and knives and frying pans made of it. Next week when we go down into town, you'll be the greatest hero, you'll see."

Gom sat up. "Knives? Frying pans?" He felt a stab of anxiety. He remembered seeing back in the gully how soft the gold had been on his finger. Even then he'd thought how useless it was for an axe blade. And now the folk were having it made into tools and utensils. It wouldn't work!

Unless—Pinkle knew about gold, didn't he? He should, being the smith and all. He'd tell them, surely, that it wouldn't work. Would persuade them to keep just to ear-rings, and chains, and such, to replace their silver trinkets. Gom nodded. The thrifty townsfolk would set great store by such lasting treasures. He relaxed, lay back, and closed his eyes. Yes, if Pinkle handled it right, all would be well.

Unless—he sat up again. Pinkle also liked to turn a profit. He might not be willing to turn away work. The fever of gold was upon the town. The townsfolk had momentarily lost their senses. That being so, the blacksmith might go ahead and do exactly what they told him to do and not let on at all. Gom let out a deep, deep breath. Far from being hailed as a hero as his father fondly thought, he had an uncomfortable feeling that some angry and disillusioned people might just be waiting to run him out of town after all!

CHAPTER TWENTY-ONE

T WAS RAINING hard when town day arrived, one week later. As they set off down the mountain, an angry Wind hurled thick sheets of fierce water in their faces. Why was Wind angry? Gom listened hard for an answer, but none came. But why should it? Wind was Wind. It didn't give a whistle for men's affairs.

Before they'd gone half a mile, Gom and his father were drenched. Before they'd gone another, the cart almost ran away from them down the slippery trail.

"You all right, son?"

Gom nodded, gulping air, spraying rivulets off the end of his chin. He'd been feeling better for three days now, but still Stig fussed over him, and would for many days more.

"You're so quiet today, son. I knew you shouldn't have left the hut so soon."

"I'm fine, Father, really I am." Gom dreaded their arrival in the town. He couldn't stop thinking of the softness of the gold, how readily it had broken between his fingers.

"Just you see," his father said, hauling on the cart to slow its descent. "You'll be the regular hero and just the fellow to brighten up the day."

In anticipation, Stig broke loudly into song, a stout declaration of Gom's brave and clever deeds. Wait until they reached town, it went. Then would Gom get his just deserts.

Gom went along, silently agreeing, fearing the dreadful reality that likely awaited them down below. Yet, he comforted himself, stumbling over a wet tree-root, catching vainly at a branch to keep himself from falling, perhaps he was being too pessimistic. Perhaps everything had worked out well. Perhaps Pinkle had added something to the gold to strengthen it, so that the folk had the pretty color and good strong tools as well. Perhaps.

He picked himself up and trudged on through wet leaf-mold and mud against the cadences of Stig's triumphal song.

* * *

All along the empty main street bubbles popped on cobbles, and the gutters ran.

Stig stopped outside the butcher's. "Come on in, Gom. Bok'll be that glad to see you, for he took a right wad of the gold to make himself a beautiful bright golden meat cleaver."

Gom shook his head, loth to test Stig's words. If Bok liked his blade so much, let him come to the door and say so. If not, well, safety lay in distance. And so he stayed by the cart, the water running off his face, dripping from his collar and down his neck. With a "Son, you're much too modest," Stig went in to strike his bargain for the week.

A moment later, Stig emerged holding something wrapped in old cloth. Avoiding Gom's eye, he threw it on top of the cart and moved quickly on down the street.

Gom, hurried alongside, full of misgiving. "What happened, Father? What's that you put on the cart? And why hasn't Bok taken any wood today?"

Stig slowed. "It's the cleaver. The blade's no good, son," he said. "It's too soft. It keeps going blunt. Bok's that mad."

Gom reached up, lifted the cloth, and looked. The blade was ragged as a split log, and its sides were pitted and scratched. There, he thought in disgust. Just as he'd expected! "But why should that make Bok mad? The gold didn't cost him a thing."

"No. But Pinkle did. He charged Bok a whole side of beef for making that blade. Bok says he'll find his own wood until the debt's paid off."

But that was terrible! Gom looked at his father aghast. What of that week's bacon, and beef dripping, and sausages, and bones for making broth? What were they going to live on?

Well, perhaps, Stig said, they'd make do with just eggs and cheese and vegetables. It wasn't the end of the world.

But they got none of those, either.

Maister Craw returned the scythe, and the spade and fork—the prongs of the fork looking like coathooks gone wrong, and Farmer Han, a pitchfork looking like a branch of corkscrew willow.

Thank goodness, Gom thought, as they hurried out of the rain to The Wild Green Man, for the bet with Gaffer Gudgeon, for they hadn't any money for elevenses that day.

Nobody was outside, of course.

"Well, look who's here!" Gaffer Gudgeon said, as Gom followed Stig into the inn parlor. "If it isn't the wizard himself and in person!" Around him, his cronies laughed.

"We've come for our first lunch," Gom said boldly,

forgetting his promise to Stig about minding his tongue. "If your word's still good."

Gaffer's smile changed to a scowl as he nodded to Winker, the host, to serve them. "There were a town meeting yesterday," Gaffer went on. "In this very parlor. It were very crowded. But I daresay you've already heard."

"No," Stig said, taking up his plate of bread and cheese and sitting down at a table near the fire. "What about?"

Gom's eyes were on Gaffer's crafty face. Why had his father fallen into the trap and asked? Now Gaffer was going to have a great good time telling them the answer, and it wasn't going to be a pleasant one.

"Oh, it were about this and that. Mostly that."

"Oh?" Stig returned Gaffer's smile. "And what was 'that'?"

Gaffer looked into his tankard. "They were deciding," he said at last, "what to tell the Queen's men when they come looking for the Royal Purrywayer."

"Which is?" Stig's smile faded some.

"Well, they thought as how since we don't know nothing about him we, er, ought to direct them, ahem, elsewhere."

Stig made a strange low sound. It was, Gom realized, the same bear growl his father had uttered down in the caves as he took on Skeller. He was getting angry! Gom began to feel afraid.

"And?"

It was clear that Gaffer didn't want to go on now, but something in Stig's voice left him no choice.

"They reckoned that them as knows are the ones to ask."

Stig stood up, pushed away his plate and beer mug.

"I suppose," he said in the sudden silence, "that you'll

all direct them up the mountain aways to a certain woodcutter's hut—no offense to the woodcutter, of course." Stig's
hands bunched into fists. "You don't fool me with your
'theys,' old man. You're a part of this town, aren't you? I
swear, Gudgeon, that if you weren't a gaffer I'd ask you to
step outside with me. And as for the rest of you—this whole
town—" Stig stared around the parlor, his face a deep dark
red. "You're cowards, all of you. And I'm sorry I brought
the gold down here, because you don't deserve it, not a
single piece.

"And as to my son, Gom—" Stig glanced to Maister
Sprogging sitting nearby. "Bagpipes aren't to everybody's
taste. There's some as dance to music of a different sort.
Just because my boy thinks different from you, there's no
call for you always to be a-picking on him. Come on, Gom,
it's time to go."

To Gom's consternation, Stig walked him away from
their full plates and frothing mugs, out into the pouring rain.

"Father," Gom said, as Stig picked up the shafts of the
cart. "What are we going to do? We haven't sold a single
log, and we've nothing in the larder for next week save the
last of the broth and some old cabbage stalks."

"Eh, I don't know, son. But I'd rather starve than eat
food growed down here. It would stick in my craw."

Gom was not so sure it would stick in his, but he said
nothing.

They moved back along the street, the pile of big gold
things chinking and rattling atop the wood. Not one door
opened. Not one housewife beckoned them over to stop and
dicker over the price of a log.

As they passed the smithy for the second time, Maister Pinkle called out. "Good day to you, Maister Stig. I'm
sorry I missed you on your way in, but I was a-sleeping late.
I'd be most obliged if you'd stop by here with your load. I

can afford to buy the whole lot today, for I've made more profit in this one week than I've made in the last two year."

Stig, brightening, pushed the cart to the smithy door, and, unloading the gold things off the top, took off the canvas cover and began to stack the logs by the side wall.

When the cart was empty, Stig rang the bell for Pinkle to come and pay him. There was a peculiar clinking sound and Pinkle appeared in the doorway, dragging along an enormous sack.

"There," he said. "That should more than enough cover the price of this load. Gold. And three more sacks of it, if you'll wait. Gold scissors, returned by Maister Corry. Wouldn't stay sharp, you see, and that's no good for a tailor, is it? Then there're all the frying pans the wives had me make. Burned the food, the gold pans did, and then got all scratched up by the scouring. And just look at these:" Pinkle picked up a tangle of twisted pokers and tongs. "Fire-irons. Quite a few folk burned themselves messing with these." He looked sideways at Gom. "You should have been here yesterday when they brought these things back. What they weren't going to do to—" He stopped. "But it don't profit nobody to speak of it now."

Gom looked at his father, but Stig only stood there dismayed, all his anger gone out of him. Well, one of them had to say something. "You're the blacksmith," Gom cried. "You must have guessed when you made these things that they wouldn't work."

Pinkle laid a finger along the side of his nose. "Maybe," he said, winking, "and maybe not. But I only done what I were paid to do. Not that I haven't had my moments. Dumped these things on my doorstep, they did. Screaming for their money back. But they didn't get it. I did the work, said I. Sweat that's paid for can't be unbought."

"I still say," Gom said, watching the blacksmith load

the gold into the cart, "that you're the one folk should be mad at, not me. I never asked them to want gold scissors and knives and such. I was thinking more of little things, of chains and earrings, and trinkets like that."

"Well," Pinkle said, as he helped strap the canvas cover back on. "Well, they didn't. For it reminded them too much of Skeller, like. No, it was tools the folk asked me for, practical as they are."

Practical! thought Gom, looking at the bulging canvas.

The blacksmith stepped back into the shelter of his smithy. "Maister Stig, take my advice, and keep yon lad home for a week or two—or longer." He laughed shortly, yet without malice. "They don't hold nothing against you, but the boy's not too popular right now." With that he disappeared into the dark of his smithy, leaving Stig and Gom looking at each other in the rain.

Stig looked back to the smithy, folding his arms.

"I'm a mite slow, and no mistake, son. But I think we've just been had." A trace of the new anger came back into his voice. He picked up one or two of the gold pieces and threw them onto the ground. "I'm blessed if we're hauling this load all the way home. They were glad enough of it when I dragged it down here. So down here it can stay."

"Nay, Father," Gom said, for a plan was forming in his mind. "It's no use dragging out trouble." He bent down and put the things back into the cart. "We'll take the gold back up the mountain where it belongs. 'Tis more fitting."

"Father! Wait!"

Gom and his father turned to look back along the street. Hilsa, a huge basket on her arm, a scarf over her head, was clattering along the wet cobbles in her heavy wooden shoes.

"Here, here, my gal, slow up." Stig took her arm, drew her under the shelter of the smithy porch. "Where are you going so fast?"

Hilsa put her hand to her chest, gasping for breath. Her face was red, maybe from her running, or from indignation, or both. "I was waiting and waiting for young Gom to come. I didn't hear the cart go by." She put the basket inside the cart and threw her arms around them both. "I think it's shameful the way folks are carrying on. Shameful!" At last she disengaged herself and lifted the cart cover. "Three loaves of bread, two dozen oatcakes, and a suet raisin pudding. It's not much, but maybe this will help too." She held up a big jar of honey. "The first from our beehives. You'll never be without honey again, Father, thanks to Gom. It were his idea we should keep bees."

Stig's face went red, then pale. "Eh, no, lass. I can't take the food from your mouth."

"Father! It's extra! There's no less in our larder. I made it all when I knowed what they were going to do today. I'm not going to speak a word to anyone until they've made things right, and that's flat. Now go along, the pair of you. You'll drown else before you're even halfway home. I'll be up to see you in three days' time, just to see how you're getting along."

Before Stig could refuse, she ruffled Gom's hair and ran off back along the street, and Gom couldn't be sure whether she was crying or whether it wasn't just the rain on her face.

Stig stood looking after her. "Well, that's a fine lass, and no mistake, to come after us like that. A fine lass."

Gom sighed. Indeed that was. Of all Stig's children, she'd been the only one to speak to them that day. "I suppose Stok had to stay inside this morning, Father," he said quietly.

"Aye, I suppose, son," Stig said, and hefting the cart handles he led the way up the trail and all the way back home. But he sang not a note one step of the way.

CHAPTER TWENTY-TWO

TIG HEATED the last of the broth for supper, but good as it smelled, Gom wouldn't take any.

"Well, we might as well have an early night tonight, son," his father said, swilling out his mug and plate in the bucket by the door.

They both undressed and lay down in their cots at either end of the hut. Stig put out the lamp at his bedside. "Don't feel too bad, my boy," he said. "It were that Skeller that started all this trouble, not you."

"Umph," said Gom. "Goodnight, Father. And Father—"

"Yes, son?"

"Sorry."

"Son, son," Stig said, then fell silent.

Gom closed his eyes, waiting for Stig to go to sleep, the Lollybob chorus going round and round inside his head:

O woe is me, for I am run out of town . . .

At the first soft snore, Gom was up and dressed.

He hadn't much to pack, had he? So it wasn't going to take him long to do what he had to do.

The rain, which had followed them all the way back up the mountain, had stopped at last. Now he could carry out the plan he'd thought of down in the town: the plan to undo the trouble he'd caused Stig, and to make sure there'd be no more of the like.

First to take the gold off his father's hands: bury it out of sight, and out of mind. Then to remove himself.

He couldn't shift the heavy cart alone, so he had to unfasten the sodden canvas cover and lift out the gold piece by piece.

Twelve trips he made into the deep of the wood, where Stig was not likely to go for many a year. There he buried the gold under a light covering of dirt and leaves. He would like to have put it back exactly where he'd found it, but he didn't have the time. At least it was where it wouldn't cause any more mischief.

When he was done, he stood looking down at the new-turned earth for a moment, thinking. Far Away that gold would probably buy his father a kingdom. Here on Windy Mountain it was a worthless nuisance.

Like him.

Gom left the cart outside the hut. "Goodbye, Father," he whispered, and walked to the far side of the clearing, wanting for one last time to tread the old familiar trail.

At the bottom, he struck out along the main street down which he and Stig had traded for so long, past the silent butcher's shop, the bakery, the greengrocery, the tailor's, the potter's, the tanner's, and the smithy porch. The sky was clear, with that special brightness it had when washed and scoured by Wind and rain. The full moon winked off the wet cobbles and cottage windows.

The Wild Green Man's courtyard was eerie in its silvery emptiness. Gom pictured the gaffers, bent over their walking sticks, cackling into their ale. He turned away and went on up the street, looking at the little houses and their neat front yards, thinking of the people sleeping within.

None of those would miss him come the morrow. None of those would sorrow over his passing. Except . . . he paused by one white picket fence, breathing in the thick heady fragrance of night roses. "Goodbye, Hilsa," he whispered. "Look after Father for me."

He looked down the road to Maister's Craw's house. Stok would be fast asleep now, in his narrow cot under the roof. What a shame he hadn't seen him that day to say goodbye. His eldest brother was sure to have been upset over the whole business, the more so because he hadn't been able to help them in any way. What would Stok think, Gom wondered, when he awoke to find Gom gone? Gom shifted uncomfortably and moved on down the moonlit street. Probably worse of him than he did now. Pity, for Stok had always been on his side. *Farewell, Stok*, he called silently. *Keep an eye out for Father, and don't think too badly of me. It's all for the best.*

Gom paused again, looking back toward the mountain peak. "It really is, Father," he said aloud. "There won't be any more trouble once I'm gone. Goodbye."

And goodbye, Hoot Owl, and Leadbelly, and Snake, and Mockingbird, and Sessery and, and everybody.

He sighed. He'd not seen one of them on his way down from the mountain, not even Hoot Owl, who usually missed nothing. It was almost as if he had not been meant to say goodbye to them at all.

He walked on resolutely to the end of the street, coming at last to Maister Craw's cabbage patch. His steps slowed, then stopped.

This was ridiculous. Where was he going? No one had ever been much farther than the end of the main street.

He must think before going on.

He turned aside, into the neat square patches of growing vegetables. All those cabbages, and carrots, and peas and beans, sitting there fat and idle, while up there Stig was going hungry. His eye caught a figure ahead, in the middle of a patch of late-sown seeds. It was big, bony big, with a broad hat and green feather, a loose tunic over its wide broomstick shoulders, and striped yellow legs like potters' chimneys. It was standing there, quite still, watching him.

Skeller!

Gom turned and ran—smack into something hard which grabbed him and held him fast. He cried out. A hand came firmly over his mouth, shutting off his cry. "Hush! Gom, whatever are you doing here?" Gom looked up in surprise—and relief. It was Stok.

Gom stared up at the tall, broad figure of his eldest brother, looking for all the world like a younger Stig, with his golden hair shining in the moonlight, his blue eyes wide in innocent surprise.

"*Nnnn, mnn-nnn-mnn,*" Gom said, struggling in his grasp. Stok took away his hand. Gom breathed deep, and smoothed down his jacket. "I'm leaving," he said. "Leaving Windy Mountain. Leaving Clack. Going Far Away." It sounded silly, put like that.

"You're what! Running away?" Stok sounded shocked. "I'd never have believed it!"

"I'm *not* running away!" Gom cried indignantly, then looked around in the darkness at the loudness of his voice.

"What did Father say?" Stok asked him.

Gom looked down at his boots. "He doesn't know, yet."

"I see," Stok said softly. "You're not running off, then. You're *sneaking* off. That's worse."

"I'm not standing here to be insulted," Gom said. "Why, *why*?" His voice rose. "Why didn't they blame Pinkle? I didn't ask them to make those stupid things, in fact I'd have told them not to. Pinkle knew, he knew that gold would be no good for ploughs and scissors and suchlike. It's his greedy fault, not mine!"

"Maybe," Stok said. "But they need Pinkle, you see, and they don't need you. So you have to be their scapegoat for a while. Don't worry. The fuss will blow over and things will return to normal again."

"No, it won't. And I'm tired of this whole town and everyone in it, except for you and Hilsa. I tell you, I'm off." He turned to walk away, but Stok caught his hand and pulled him back.

"You'll kill Father," he said. "He'll never recover. You're his sun and moon and four seasons. You go, and his world will stop."

"I don't think so," Gom said. "I'm just a thorn in his side. He'll get on much better without me. He'll get the peace and quiet he deserves."

"Maybe," Stok said, "but there'd be no point, don't you see? Anyway, I heard what happened today, and his speech in The Wild Green Man is the talk of the town. No one's ever seen Stig angry. He's gained much respect in everyone's eyes. There's also a lot of feeling against Gaffer Gudgeon, over what he said and the way he said it. And there's talk against Pinkle as well, for being so grasping, and for cheating Stig out of his wood with the gold."

While Stok was speaking, Gom remembered his fright and glanced over to where he'd seen the ghostly figure standing looking at him.

Stok caught his glance. "Oh, meet Sir Dismas," he said.

"Rather fine, don't you think? Made him myself and stuck him out here four days ago. There's not been a single crow on the field since!"

Stok drew Gom closer, close enough to see the broad-brimmed hat, the jaunty feather in its side; the velvet smock, and the bright striped pants.

"Where," he whispered, stiffening, "did you get the clothes?" He pictured the last time he'd seen Skeller's hat, and where he'd buried it.

"Oh—didn't anyone tell you? You know that horse of his—what was his name?"

"Pinosquat," said Gom.

"That's it, Pinnysquat, or something. Well, they found him in a hay barn. Practically eaten his way through it he had. So stuffed they couldn't get him out the door. Anyway, to cut a long story short, Skeller's pack was still on him, mostly full of things the townsfolk had traded him. We opened it up and gave everybody back the things belonging to them. Farmer Han is going to keep the horse so's his old mare can take a rest. Make that patchwork nosebag do some honest work for the first time in his life. And I took this spare set of clothes, including this fine spare hat—Skeller won't be needing them anymore, will he?—and here we are. Say hello to Gom, Sir Dismas," he called softly to the figure. "Show your manners, for once!"

Gom relaxed. It was a scarecrow, a fine scarecrow—but one he'd just as soon not see any closer. Then he stiffened again, this time with anger. "A bunch of hypocrites, that's what this town is, that would set the Queen's soldiers on Father and me over Skeller getting himself killed, while picking his things over like hungry buzzards!"

"Hey, hey, that's me you're talking about, too." Stok drew Gom over to a grassy bank, made him sit down beside him. "We only took back what was ours, little brother, and maybe a bit extra for compensation. Look," Stok went on, "I know how you must feel right now. And I know how lonely you must be up there with only Father. *And* I know I've not been the best of brothers to you, for I've never known how. You're not the easiest person in the world to please, you must admit. But at least in me—and Hilsa too—you have *somebody*. Which is better than nobody. Which is all you'll have Far Away."

"That's not the point," Gom said. "It's not just the trouble over the gold that's bothering me. Folk don't like me, and that's always made things awkward for Father. Today was the very worst. Then there's how poor we are. Father hasn't even a decent jacket for this coming winter. There's never enough to last the week, and Father always goes without on account of me. He'll be much better off alone."

"Oh no, he won't," Stok said. "We're going round in circles, Gom. You're the one who doesn't understand. Without you, Stig won't care whether he eats or not. And if he ever thought you'd gone because of him, he'd never forgive himself.

"Gom: as you're Mother's son—and more so than the rest of us—there has to be an itch in you to get out of here. I for one am surprised you haven't shown it before. But as you're Father's son, you have a duty to stick by him. Especially now. He's not getting any younger, you know. Who's going to look after him when his work gets too much for him?"

Gom stared. Stig *old*? Why, the idea was absurd.

"You're a son of a woodcutter, whatever our mother was. That woodcutter's raised you, loved you, and protected you. You can't run out on him now he needs you.

"Also, you belong here. When Father's gone, Clack'll need another woodcutter—and that's you, just as when Maister Craw's gone, I'm to be greengrocer in his place. It's our duty, you see. We all have duties to others as you should know, only I daresay Father's never bothered your head with such talk."

Gom still stared at his brother. No. His father hadn't. And why should he? Why should Gom feel any duty toward those closed, opinionated, smug, self-righteous—

"Look, Gom," Stok went on, "without Clack, our father'd never have made his living as a woodcutter all these years. He'd never have been able to provide for his children as long as he did, and there'd have been no one to take nine of them at least off his hands. Everything we do, everything we have, and everything we are is thanks to somebody else. We don't live in a hole, you see. We owe, and we're owed. Maister Craw took me in, gave me a good home, and I work hard to pay him back and to be a credit to him and to the town." Stok looked down. "I'm to be wed come the fall," he said. "Ditty Wimble's promised me her hand."

Gom said nothing. He thought Ditty Wimble a particularly thick and stupid wench who'd never done anything more to Gom than put her hands on her fat hips and stare at him as though he were a—a frog in a jar, but if Stok thought fit to wed her that was his affair.

He scratched his head.

Stok's words made some sense. Maybe he was wrong running away. He wasn't exactly prepared for going Far Away. Why, all he knew was Windy Mountain, and how to cut wood and make boxes. And what of his friends up there? What would Hoot Owl and Leadbelly say when they learned that Gom had run off? A new and awful thought then suddenly occurred to him: what of Stig? *What would his father do when for the second time in his life he woke to find someone he loved and counted on, gone?* "Maybe going Far Away isn't such a great idea after all," he muttered.

Stok caught the words. "It certainly isn't. Think, Gom. That Skeller, who caused all this, he came from Far Away. You've never met such evil as that here in Clack. No, sir."

That was true, thought Gom. Suddenly, he saw the folly of what he'd been going to do. To run off, into—what? Terrible evils, probably. Among folk ten times worse than Gaffer or Bok or Pinkle at cheating a body out of a bargain, and he as simple out there as ever Stig was in the town.

Stig. His father. Stig without a son to care for him and to carry on his work when he no longer could. How glad he was that he had bumped into Stok just then. Which raised a question in his mind. "What," he asked his brother, "are you doing out here in the middle of the night? Has the old man got you working all twenty-four hours now?"

Stok laughed. "Not exactly. I'm here on what you might call, unofficial business. Come and see." He led Gom down one of the pathways between raspberry and blackcurrant bushes until he came to a large bulging sack lying on the ground. In it were potatoes, and carrots, and spinach, and cabbage, and lettuce and tomatoes, and cucumbers and apples and pears, and round, ripe berries crowning the lot in a nest of straw. "For you and Father," he said. "I was just about to bring them up to leave outside your door. Maister Craw won't miss them for once."

Gom stared. He'd never seen so much wonderful food. He looked up into Stok's face. "You're a good son," he said. "You and Hilsa are both good children to Father. Much better than I could ever be."

"Rubbish." Stok bent down and unfolded a second sack. "Here, young 'un, give us a hand. Now we can both go up there together."

Gom held the sack open, watched Stok divide the load between them. How kind of Stok, to have gotten up out of his bed in the middle of the night like that. Gom hung his head. He himself had gotten up only to bring his father sorrow and woe.

He was quiet all the time they refilled the sacks and tied them up, all the way back through the back alleys to the mountain track.

But when they were up aways above the roofs of the sleeping town, Gom's face lightened, and finally curved into a smile. "I think," he said, "I'll sing a tune or two to help us along. For these sacks are so heavy, and as Father always says, the way is always easier for a song."

CHAPTER TWENTY-THREE

Y THE TIME they reached the hut it was too late for Stok to stay. He had to be back down the mountain before Maister Craw woke up. So it fell to Gom alone to tell his father the next morning about how he'd almost run away, and how he'd met Stok in the cabbage patch. How Stok had crept out in the middle of the night to pick food for them, and how he and Gom had brought it back up the trail. "You should have seen us, Father. It was still so slippery, that we had to take the really steep parts on the run, and on some of the long stretches we'd come to a full stop and stagger backwards until we got to the bottom and we'd have to climb all over again. We really could've used one of your ropes!"

Stig was not so merry, not even at the sight of the food. "What if you hadn't met Stok, son? Would you really have gone?"

Gom thought for a minute, feeling ashamed at the hurt

look in his father's eyes. "No, Father. I couldn't have left you, not in the end. That's why I stopped and turned aside in the first place. It was just something I had to get out of my system, that's all. I'm that glad to be home again, I can tell you. Isn't this where I belong?"

"Maybe, son. I hope so, anyway," Stig replied. But Gom sensed there was much left unsaid.

The week went by. As each day passed, Stig seemed to grow cheerier and more at ease with Gom. Yet through that week, Gom found himself watching Stig hefting the mighty axe blade, swinging it again and again with great force into the trunks of hard, resisting trees, feeling the impact of steel on wood as if it were his own body doing the work. And all the time he wondered if here, or there, his father didn't look a little strained, or pained, or stiff: whether it wasn't taking him longer to load the logs or split the wood and pull it back to the hut.

On the fourth day following the runaway affair, Stig, bringing down a particularly hard tree, pulled his back and only with great difficulty finished his work and returned home.

"If you hadn't been there to help me, son," Stig said to Gom, as later they sat by the fire—Stig strapped in a mustard plaster—"I'd still be out there under the stars, all seized up and unable to move a step!"

Gom pooh-poohed his father's words, yet in his heart, he heard their truth.

That night, he tossed and turned, unable to sleep. He lay in the light of the dying fire, staring at the door. Stok was right, he told himself. Father needs me, and will need me more. And here I am, gadding about the mountainside after my own petty affairs. It's time I really set to work and stopped playing around.

On that thought, he sighed deeply and tossed about to face the wall. But sleep still wouldn't come. His thoughts drifted to the townsfolk down below. Wasn't it time he made his peace with them, too? On his very next visit he'd learn to make himself useful so that they'd accept him at last—nay, even need him. That way, he'd be a credit to his father and not an embarrassment. Relieved, he turned over to face the door again. But still sleep wouldn't come.

In the wake of all the fuss over the gold and Skeller, Gom's thoughts had been turning again and again to the strange waking dream he'd had of the skull under the mountain. The temptation to return to Sessery's halls to seek it, and the answers to its mystery had been almost overwhelming at times during those following days. Because it was connected with his mother's rune in some way—or to his mother herself! He was sure now that the visions had not come from the Wife. The gold had brought nothing but trouble and disaster, which the Wife could not possibly have wished upon husband and son. No. The vision of the gold must have come from the skull somewhere within the mountain, and with it, danger. Gom sat up in bed. The rune had been not inviting him to find the gold—but warning him against it!

He lay back again. What a fool he was, over and over again. When would he ever grow wise?

How he longed to go at once to the limestone caverns to find that skull and have a reckoning. But he was turning over a new leaf, and putting his old ways behind him.

Gom sighed. He'd surely miss his old haunts. Too bad. Tomorrow he'd make his fresh start, make a clean, clear break from his old life.

He sat up again. Before he made this clean, clear break there was one thing left to do. He crept out of bed, dressed, and dragged the cart through the woods to where he'd buried the gold. This was not its proper resting place. This stuff that had brought death and set men against one another had come from under the very roots of the mountain. To close that whole wretched episode he must return that bright and shining metal to its source. He'd not had time the night he ran away. But he had now. He dug it up and loaded it onto the cart.

Hoo! called Hoot Owl. "And where might you be going, Spindleshanks, who should be a-bed getting yourself ready for work tomorrow, instead of rousting the whole neighborhood out with your racket and scaring off people's suppers?"

"To the limestone caverns," Gom said, without stopping.

"*Again!* Wasn't there enough commotion over that the other night? What for now?"

"I'm taking this stuff back where it belongs," Gom answered him, and hoisting the cart shafts, he trundled on over fern and moss, the cart behind him swaying and bumping and twisting in his grasp as though it were a wild beast struggling to escape.

Cartload by cartload, he wheeled the ruined treasure to Sessery's front door. Armful by armful, he carried it under the mountain through Sessery's front door; over the crevasse, through the cave of stalactites and stalagmites, and on to the broken ledge where Skeller had fallen to his death. He was so eager to be rid of the gold that it took him less than an hour to transfer it all and toss it over. At the last load, Gom leaned over and called, "There, now. You have your treasure at last. Sleep in peace!"

He stood, listening to his echoes dying away: *Sleee . . . p . . . eeee . . . p . . . eeee . . . p . . . eee . . .*

eeeeeeeeace. And went very, very still. There was something about those echoes. He called again, loud and long, listening once more to the sounds dying away. *Yo . . . o . . . oho . . . oooooooooooooo. . . .*

The old familiar excitement of discovery stirred within him.

Gom wet his finger, dangled his arm down above the broken ledge where Stig had wrestled with Skeller, and felt a definite draft on it. To the left, and to the right, a layer of tunnels ran beneath him; another gallery, newly exposed, below the one on which he now stood. He remembered the amber light shining through solid rock, along a tunnel he'd never seen before. And the skull. His excitement grew.

How long had those tunnels been sealed up? For long, and Gom had never once detected them. But Stig's subsidence had crashed right through that layer, opening those tunnels up, and in the heat of all the danger and trouble, Gom had not even noticed.

"Sessery?"

MMMMmmmmm?

"Why didn't you tell me there were more tunnels under here?"

Mmmmmmmmnn, you never asked.

"How far do they go? And where do they come out?"

There was no reply.

He stayed there for a minute or two, looking down. Then he remembered his resolution. Time to move, he told himself guiltily. Hadn't he resolved to leave this all behind him? Wasn't this why he'd thrown the gold down there in the first place, to make a clear and clean new start?

He stood up to go, then hesitated, reluctant to move. The skull *was* down there, he just knew it! If he walked away out of there his mind would know no rest. Unanswered questions would always remain to bother him, like an itch unscratched. Maybe, he persuaded himself, this urge to go below to find it was part of the ending. Maybe this one last discovery was a necessary step in turning his back on Sessery's domain, leaving his old way of life for good.

As if in answer to his thoughts, there came a faint tingling against his chest!

Quickly, Gom slipped over the edge of the cave-in and climbed down the rock-face, spiderlike, working along to the left.

Gom didn't have to go far to reach the newly exposed tunnel floor. Gingerly, he let his weight down onto it. It held. He stood for a minute, feeling the rune's vibrations growing stronger, half-expecting the strange amber glow to appear. Nothing happened. He edged farther along the tunnel until the floor ended abruptly. Beyond was only space stretching down and down.

So much for going left.

He went back to his starting place and struck out again, this time to the right, feeling his way slowly, alert for more subsidence and sudden space. As he went the feeling grew on him that something or someone was drawing him as surely as a beckoning finger.

He called out, listened to the echoes.

The tunnel was nearing a dead end.

Gom's nose began to tickle. How dusty the air was in that place. For how many ages, he wondered, had it lain undisturbed until unsealed by the violence on the ledge?

The rune was almost humming now, and the feeling of being drawn was overwhelming. "Hello . . . ho," he called softly. There was no reply. But the sound of his voice told him that he now stood in a small cave.

With his fingertips he traced rough, close walls and a low, arched roof. Along the back of the cave was a raised ledge, high as a workbench, and wide as a bed. The dust lay thick and not pleasant to the touch. His questing fingers closed on something cold and smooth. A small stone jar. A metal dish. A bottle. Unstoppered. Empty, lying on its side. And—his eyes widened in the darkness—an oil lamp.

He picked it up, shook it.

Still half full.

Gom let go the rune and from his back pocket pulled out a flint.

On the third try the lampwick caught, and flared, filling the hollow space with brilliance. Then it sputtered and died, and wouldn't light again.

No matter.

In the brief glare he'd seen everything in that place: the dusty jar, blue under the smears left by his fingertips; rotted bales; the upturned bottle; a broken dish.

And something else.

Setting down the lamp he reached out and touched what he sought. Then he closed both hands upon it, turned it all about. It was light and smooth, hard and curved, grooved, and hollow as death.

The skull.

Carefully, Gom set it down, felt around for the other bones lying on that stone ledge, on the rotted stuff that must have served as mattress, in the rotted threads that must have served as clothes.

Who had the skeleton been? And how had it gotten down there? It had certainly been down there a very, very long time.

Funny, Gom thought, but now he had found it he didn't

feel in the least afraid. Rather he thought he understood. He'd been right. The skull, not the rune, had drawn him to the gold. He was being asked a favor, he was certain of it. And the gold had been offered him in advance payment!

But the rune's vibrations—what had they to do with either? Had the stone been trying to warn him away from the offer? Or. . . . He caught his breath. His mother had disappeared on the day he was born. Gone away, his father thought. What if she'd come down here and had an accident—what if these bones were hers! That would certainly explain the rune's coming alive every time he saw the skull.

No. If she'd had an accident, she'd never have taken off the rune and deliberately left it with him. Besides, the tunnels had been sealed up until a few days ago. And—he picked up a bone—his mother was short: surely these bones were large. Or were they?

He shook himself. You can't stay here forever, he said. You have a job to do.

There was a moldy sack lying folded in one corner. Gom carefully rolled the bones up in it, all of them save the skull. This he would have to come back for, because his arms—and the sack—were full.

With great care, he picked up the bundle and made his way back up the tunnel. He climbed the rock wall above the broken ledge, and went back through the cavern of stalagmites and stalactites, over the chasm, into Sessery's wide front hall, and out into the open at last. There he set the bones down, still rolled in the sack, and went back for the skull.

Sessery wafted past, amused at his comings and goings.

"I've found the remains of someone," he told her. "I'm going to bury them outside. Do you know who it was?" He waited for answer, holding his breath.

Sessery whirled lightly about his head and blew gently in his ear.

A man there was for long, she whispered. *Not like you, not a quick little thing like you. Tall, he was, and . . . still. One day he came into that cave, and sat. And there he sat, scarcely ever going out. Just sat, until the day he died; sometimes with the light on, mostly not, because I'd blow it out, for fun. That's all.*

Gom let out his breath. "When? How long ago?"

Sessery rose into the air, whistled through the stalactites spiking the tunnel roof. *When? What does that mean? He came. He stayed. And would stay yet but for you stirring his bones. Bones. Agh! Such rigid things they are. He's much better . . . without . . . them.* Her voice soared away, up to the higher galleries and Gom heard her no more that night.

He sighed and went on down.

Back in the cave, he went to the bench to take up the skull. Sessery said it had been that of a man. "There, old fellow," he said quietly, reaching out. "So many of my summer friends I've buried under the stars. I can surely do as much for you."

Gom's fingers touched the skull and at once they burned as though they had touched a pot on the fire. He started back, pressing himself into the wall. The image of the skull began to waver and blur about the edges, then light up with an inner radiance; a lovely, warm and amber glow.

He blinked, shook his head a little as if to clear it. When he looked again, the skull was gone and in its place was the head of a man.

CHAPTER TWENTY-FOUR

HAT A WONDROUS head it was! The forehead was high, and wide, topped with a mass of gray-black hair. Thick, black eyebrows arched finely over a long, thin nose whose bridge, steep-angled, shone in the light. The jaw, narrow and also very long, was covered by a great bushy beard, while the eyes—the eyes! They were gray, deep shadowed; wise and very, very sad.

Who are you?

"The name's Gom. Gom Gobblechuck, the woodcutter's son," Gom said. "I've a mind that you've been calling me."

Your mind tells you right, Gom Gobblechuck. I've been expecting you.

"To bury you, I think."

Partly. I've been down here too long. I would lie beneath the stars.

"It just so happens," Gom said promptly, "that I've the

very place for you. A mulberry tree as wide as any you ever saw, by a high waterfall. The water sings all the year round, even in the deep winter freeze, and come the spring, the new leaves pop lacy as doilies and the new-melted snow chatters down from the peak. But—who are *you*, and how did you come here?"

They called me, Mandrik, and I came from Far Away. The dark eyes glittered. *I was a merchant once. I had great wealth and power, and I enjoyed the favor of queens and kings. But at the last I grew tired of commerce and the pomp of worldly affairs. I walked away from it all and took refuge here, seeking the richer realms within the mind.*

"Oh. How wonderful. And interesting," Gom said. To think that such an important person would leave the great Far Away for Windy Mountain!

The mouth twisted wryly.

Not so wonderful. And not so interesting. A fool's a fool alone as in a crowd. That I learned too late. Before I could go home, I fell sick and died. After all this time, burial with my kin has lost meaning. But I would, as I've said, like to feel starlight on my grave. Mandrik fixed Gom with a keen stare.

Gom's hand went to the rune. He pulled it out, without thinking, and turned it about in his fingers. So he had been right: the gold was Mandrik's gift, not the rune's— disastrous gift indeed. But the man had meant well, so he would not tell him of it. Instead, Gom said, "Thank you for the gold, but there was no need. I would have buried you for nothing."

Mandrik's heavy eyebrows went up. *The gold? You think it came from me? Young man, think again.*

"But—who, then?"

Your mother, your mother, boy. She, it was, who would

have you find it. Come closer. Show me what you have in your hand.

Dazed, Gom stepped forward and held out the rune. *His mother!*

That's it. Now turn it slowly. Good. The eyes half closed as Mandrik examined its curious markings. *Ten years, it is, since I last saw that stone.* The eyes suddenly opened wide. *Young man, do you know to whom it belongs!*

"Why, to me. My mother left it by me when she—went away."

Yes, yes. But do you know who she is!

"Do I—" Gom stared.

Obviously not. Turn the stone again until I say. That's it. Now . . . stop! See those curly lines running around the edge from top to bottom! That is her name. The rest I can't read, for they are magical signs that give the name its power.

His mother's name. Then he'd been right! This was writing. His mother was a wizard, just as he'd guessed. "What is the name? What does it say?" Gom stepped even closer in his excitement, thrusting the stone practically under Mandrik's nose.

It says "Harga the Brown." Mandrik's mouth curved into a smile. *You look just like her, you know.*

"I do?" As many times as Stig had told him this, Gom felt strongly affected by Mandrik's words. He looked away from Mandrik unable to speak.

She didn't tell me her name, of course, Mandrik went on. *She wouldn't, to keep whole the rune's power. But I knew her as soon as I saw her. She is a legend out there.*

Gom turned back to Mandrik. "You say you saw this stone only ten years ago? You can't have, for you've been down here much longer than that."

Mandrik smiled gravely. *You not only look like her, but you have a touch of her mind. Your mother came down here many times. How, I cannot tell you. She found my remains, and gave me power to speak with her—it is only through her that I appear to you like this.* The gray eyes went dreamy. *Many times we spoke of life and—things. The last time I saw her, she told me that she was going away. She asked me to watch for you around this time, and to show you the gold. She wanted you to find it, to make of it what you would. What did you make of it, by the way?*

Gom, suddenly realizing the implications of Mandrik's words, stepped backward. "That's a lie!" he cried. "That gold brought Father and me nothing but trouble and sorrow. If my mother is a wizard, she would have known that. She would never have wished such upon her own family!"

Mandrik's mouth twisted. *You think not? I repeat— what did you make of it, young man? Tell me, for I would know what lesson she would have you learn.*

The gray eyes looked steadily into Gom's angry dark ones. Gom's anger subsided suddenly and he found himself telling Mandrik everything. Of how he had gone into the gully to find the frog. How he had found the flakes instead. "Though you already know about that," he said. "And the vision of the gold lumps." He told of Skeller, and the way the man had sought to kill him. Of Stig going under the mountain, and Skeller's death. He told about the fiasco down in the town and his failed attempt to run away. And lastly, of his own change of heart, and his efforts to bury the past and begin again. "So now the gold's gone. I've put it back more or less where I found it. I'm setting my past behind me, seeking to please my father by becoming a proper woodcutter's son. And that's the whole awful tale."

Gom looked to Mandrik, waiting for him to speak. But the gray eyes regarded Gom fixedly while the silence lengthened.

So. Mandrik spoke at last. *You had no use for the gold, then. It's all over with it, I suppose.*

Gom nodded. "Yes. And evil, and thoughts of Far Away." Absently, he turned the rune over and over between his fingers.

Mandrik smiled. *You think that since it proved a worthless nuisance here, it were best buried! Is that what your mother wanted you to learn!*

Gom considered. *That could be.*

Fool! Mandrik cried, his voice suddenly harsh. *What lesson is that! No! This is what she would have you learn: bury a thing of great price and you deserve to lose it! Out there in the wide world, gold buys not cabbages, but kings!*

Gom frowned. "I don't understand," he said.

Mandrik's voice went soft again. *No more you should. That is why Harga had you find the gold. Listen: as you are your mother's true son, you have gold within you of far greater value than that yellow stuff you tossed down after that ruffian. Gold that cannot remain buried within you here. You must take your treasure from Windy Mountain where it never will be recognized, and out into the wide world. That is what Harga would have you learn from the gold.* The lips parted into a sudden smile. *The extra lesson from that rogue Skeller was an unforeseen bonus— or was it, knowing Harga . . .*

"An extra lesson?"

If you must take your inner wealth out there, take care to keep it close, showing it to no man until you are sure he's not another Skeller.

"But what wealth? And where would I take it?"

You will know, given a little thought. Your way lies far. Through dangers and hardships, no doubt. And for a purpose perhaps known only to Harga.

Gom's heart beat fast. "Mandrik, I believe you now, even though I do not yet fully understand you. But it hurts to think that my mother could have brought such trouble upon my father and me. Such a strong lesson it was—even cruel."

The gray eyes flashed. *You think the roads out there are lined with cradles, and blankets to wrap you in? Young man, you have watched the creatures up on this mountain raise their young. Do you think them cruel, bringing up their offspring hard, to teach them to survive?*

Gom looked down. "I suppose not." He felt foolish. Harga's son or no, he wasn't making a very good showing in front of Mandrik. "This is all so sudden," he said. "And strange. Can you tell me anything more about my mother? And—and the rune? You say it has some of her power. I have felt it, many times. Vibrating, like now. Times like this I can almost hear it humming. Here, let me put it to your ear."

Nay, Mandrik said. *That would be of no use. The stone sings only for those who are meant to hear.* The gray eyes glittered. *Take my advice, boy. Remember Skeller. Show neither your own treasure or that rune until you're sure of your company. As for the rune—there are those who would bear that token ill will, and him who wears it for Harga.*

Gom, frowning, twisted the rune's leather thong in his fingers. "Why? Is my mother—bad?"

No. Certainly not. She is good—for a wizard. She is perhaps the most powerful wizard in all the world—though you must never repeat that aloud out there if you would stay alive.

"Why?"

Why? The wide mouth curled into a smile. *Harga is of the Brown Order.*

"Brown Order?" Gom asked, but the gray eyes were closing.

Your way lies over the mountains, Mandrik said. His voice had grown weary. *That is part of your lesson. Oh, you'll stay on here as long as your father needs you, doing your duty as a good son should. But after that! Go seek your mother. Wizards don't give away their runes, but only loan them for a while—even to their children.* He laughed softly. *Most put out, your mother'll be, if she has to come all the way back here to fetch it.*

Gom glanced down at the rune. Go to seek his mother? He began to feel dizzy.

Mandrik opened his eyes wide, fixing them for a last time on Gom. *I wish you great good luck. You'll need it.* The lids fluttered shut. *I am spent. I'll sleep now. My good wishes go with you, Gom Gobblechuck, son of Harga the Brown. Farewell.*

The light shimmered, blurring the fine outlines of the head. Then faded, leaving only a dim glow from the aged skull. Then it died, leaving Gom in the dark.

It was some time before Gom took up the skull. He did so gingerly, remembering the shock he'd gotten from it last time. But it felt dead, lifeless. He stood with it for a few moments, feeling its dryness, its brittleness, its very antiquity. Then he took it with the greatest respect away down the passage, up and out under the starlight.

* * *

The hole under the mulberry tree was deep and dry,

dug with a spade fetched from the back of the hut. Gom had also brought with him a small cedar box from the back of the woodshed, and into this he carefully arranged the bones, topping them with the skull. He closed the lid, and was just about to place the box into the hole when he got up again and began casting about in the undergrowth. Presently satisfied, he bent once more and raised the lid of the box.

"There, Mandrik, sir," he said softly. "It's not much, but it's the best I can do at short notice." And with that, he laid in the box a briar rose, a sprig of mint, two jay's feathers, a handful of cob-nuts, then, on second thought, he added the golden loder leaf and lastly, in a rush of good-will, his precious insect in the stone.

"Sleep well, Mandrik, and farewell." He closed the lid a second time, lowered the box into the hole and replaced the earth. Then, his mind full of all that Mandrik had told him, he wandered off back home.

* * *

His father was standing at the door in his nightshirt, a lantern in his hand.

"Son, son! Where have you been?" His face looked ashen in the yellow lamplight.

Gom opened his mouth to tell, then changed his mind. Hadn't he stirred his father up enough already? What with the gold and Skeller, and the fuss down in the town. And his almost running away. It had wounded his father more deeply than ever he could have realized. Hilsa had told him on their last visit how Stig had sat looking out for the Wife day after day when Gom had been born. "Don't blame yourself, Gom dear," she'd said, hugging him to her. "You worn't to know. But when the bottom has dropped out of a man's life once, he's bound to be leery of it happening again. He'll get over it, in time." Gom hung his head in shame. He'd known, had known that night standing in the cabbage patch with Stok.

"I've been out walking, Father. I got too hot and stuffy lying there. I wanted to clear my head a bit." Well, that was true. He took the lantern from Stig and went inside, angry with himself. How stupid, not to think that his father would wake and find him gone and fear that he'd run off again. The fire was still warm. He kicked the ashes and blew on the embers. "Let's have a cup of tea, Father. And some toast. Walking about and thinking works one up a fearful appetite!"

It was almost dawn when he finally lay down in his bed. He'd made light of his walk, had told Stig some preposterous tales of what he'd seen under the trees, and Stig at Gom's request had sung the comical ballad of the amorous quail.

"Hardly worth getting ourselves down, son," Stig said, putting out the lamp at last. "I think for once we'll let old man cardinal wake up the day on his own!"

Gom, laughing, agreed. But the laugh did not go deep. How he longed to tell his father about Harga and the rune and Mandrik. But his father would only start fretting over the Wife all over again. And if Stig was worried now about Gom leaving him, how would he feel if Gom told him what Mandrik said? *Your way lies over the mountains.*

No, he must keep that episode to himself, telling no one. Not Stig, not Hilsa, not Stok. No one. He turned over restlessly. He was tired, so tired. But he didn't sleep, for Mandrik's words went through and through his head: *You must take your treasure from Windy Mountain . . . and out into the wide world. That is what Harga would have you learn. . . .*

*   *   *

From the next day on, Gom was true to his resolution, setting himself to work to become a good son and a credit to Stig.

If he did visit Sessery still from time to time it was rarely and with the greatest discretion. Oft-times, though, he took to sitting under the mulberry, turning the rune over in his hands, staring at the markings on the stone as though they might tell him their mystery. But to his great vexation, he couldn't even be sure now which squiggles had spelled out Harga's name. So much for being his "mother's true son"!

Summer faded into fall, and with it the excitement of that night's encounter. Thoughts of Far Away grew dim, and his world shrank once more to the limits of Windy Mountain. But every now and then something would stir his blood to restlessness and thoughts of what might lie beyond the horizon.

Gom was passing by the mulberry tree late one afternoon when Wind blew through, lifting the dying leaves, shaking them gently to earth.

Gom raised his head and sniffed. There was a strange smell in the clearing he'd never noticed before. A sweet, tangy smell. Fresh, and rotten, and salty, all at once.

Why, that's the smell of the sea, Wind told him. *I thought I'd bring you a little back, seeing as how you keep looking yonder.*

The sea? What was that?

Why, it's a great salt creek, almost as big as the whole

world, Wind said. *A restless, rolling, rollicking, roiling, boiling body of water that's never still. And in it live creatures that you'd never dream of. You must go and see them some day for yourself.*

"How far away is it?" Gom asked, but Wind had already gone, over the little stream, and on. So Gom simply sat and thought about the sea, and what else lay beyond the mountain. Once he'd thought that the mountain was the whole world, until Hoot Owl had put him right. "This little pile of rock on which you are so perilously perched," Hoot Owl said, "is no more than a pimple on the great face of the world. Even I, who've never flown farther than your eye can see, knows that. Why, there are vast wonders out there of which I can't conceive, and I'm much wiser than you!"

Well, obviously this *sea* was one. And when next he spoke with Wind, he asked more about it. And about other matters, too. About life, and how each body came to be its own self.

Simple, Wind murmured in reply. *Take me, for instance. My breath blows different tunes through different places, while in itself it remains the same. At one and the same breath from me, some things bow, some break; some things scatter and multiply, while others are destroyed. With that same breath I bear some things aloft, others I sweep into a hole. That same breath is welcome to some; by others, shunned. And yet, as I said, it's the one breath. Within myself I am constant. I am what I am. I go my way, let each thing make of me what it will.*

"That's good!" Gom cried. "That's how I'll be. Whatever folk say of me in future, good or bad, I'll not heed, but just stay true to myself!"

And as he said that, he thought of the gold flake that

he still kept in his pouch. A gift from Harga, as he now came to think of it. Prized by some, useless to others; valued and valueless. The same gold. The same flake. It was folks's attitudes that differed. How wise his mother was, and how clever to teach him that lesson long after she had gone away.

All through the autumn days, Gom toiled alongside Stig, even wielding the large axe when his father got tired, and in the end surprised himself with his own strength. More and more he did the heavy work like stacking big logs, and loading the cart, although Stig always insisted on taking that cart down into town.

"You're a fine son," Stig said to him one morning, when the tang of frost lay on the air. Gom's birthday, it was, eleven years to the day on which the Wife had disappeared; and as clear and sharp and sunny as that very one had been. "A father couldn't wish for better. And a fine woodcutter you're turning out to be."

Gom nodded and smiled, but when his father wasn't looking, he glanced up past the mountain peak, beyond the rim, to where the treetops bled into the sky. He would never leave Stig. Over there somewhere was Far Away, and the sea, and queens and kings and great cities . . . and Harga the Brown. He looked down into the mists huddling over the valley and sighed. Mandrik had said he'd leave one day, but Gom couldn't see it.

* * *

The seasons slowly came and went. At last Stig's fine yellow thatch turned completely white, his blue eyes faded and grew weak, and his voice wavered in the wind. But as ever, he still insisted on doing the main work outside, felling and chopping, and wheeling the cart down into the town, Gom pulling a smaller one now to lighten the load, until one deep winter snowfall blocked the track. . . .

III

CHAPTER TWENTY-FIVE

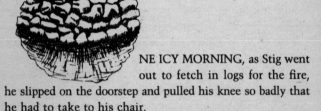

NE ICY MORNING, as Stig went out to fetch in logs for the fire, he slipped on the doorstep and pulled his knee so badly that he had to take to his chair.

Gom worked hard that day, fetching the water from the pump, making all the meals, washing their clothes, kneading poultices for Stig's knee.

Stig fretted at having to sit all the time, until Gom suggested he carve himself a walking stick so that he could get about the hut.

"Good idea," said Stig, brightening up. "And if it turns out well, I'll make more to take down into the town for the gaffers."

Gom went outside and rooted out from the woodpile a stout ash stick with a large knot in it that would with work make a very fine handle. Stig took it, rapped it on the hearth and nodded. "I shall put my best effort into this," he said. "The handle shall be a sparrow; and all up and down it shall run the friends you and I have made over the years, and for shelter they'll have oak leaves and wild vine."

Gom watched his father setting himself to work, pleased to see his spirits raised again. But they didn't stay raised for long. That very night, they sat by the hearth while about them Wind blew fresh snow, piling it up against the walls, then whisking it away again over the brittle trees. Gom was making a little cedar box inlaid with leaves and flowers of pinewood, and Stig was working on his stick. So cozy they were, thought Gom. Just like the old times. Or so he thought, until Stig put aside his knife and sighed deeply.

"I'm that worried, son. I don't hardly know what to do."

Gom looked at his father in surprise. "Why, Father? What about?"

Stig rubbed his bad knee. "I'm not getting any younger, you know, though I can't complain."

"Rubbish, Father. You're ever the man you were, and will be for many a year."

"Maybe. But that's not the point. To speak plain, son, it's you that's bothering me. When I'm gone, I don't know what'll become of you."

Gom looked up sharply. Every so often, Stig would come out with a remark that made Gom wonder if his father didn't know much more than he ever let on. Gom had never spoken of that far night under the mountain, had never since made much of Harga's rune—had never even spoken of his mother at all unless Stig mentioned her first. But for all this had Stig guessed Gom's sometime thoughts more than Gom had realized?

"Become of me, father? Am I not a woodcutter's son?

If ever a body had a trade, it's I. And there'll never be a shortage of customers down in Clack. Come on, this is glum talk of a cheerful winter's evening."

"Not glum. Disquieted, more like. My heart's not at rest, you see. Every time I think about it, I'm minded of your mother, and how like her you are; and yet not like, for I see you gallivanting Far Away and coming to a sticky end because for all your smartness you're still but a simple mountain boy and ignorant of the great wide world out there. Gom: promise me you'll stay here and lead a sensible life and be a credit to yourself and me, then I'll rest happy."

Gom looked into his father's eyes, saw pain and worry. "If it sets your mind at ease, I promise, Father. Though there's no need, you know."

"That's what I told myself, and yet—" Stig stopped, took up his carving knife, and began to sing: "There was a jolly woodman who had a son," and Gom knowing that tune well, joined in, and with that they sang themselves far into the evening and happily off to bed.

But as Gom fell asleep that night, he looked around the firelit walls thinking of the promise he'd made to Stig: to do what his father expected; to do what the town expected. To stay and carry on life as his father had before him.

He turned over.

Your way lies over the mountain. . . . Oh, you'll stay on here as long as your father needs you. . . . But after that! Go seek your mother. . . .

It was many hours that night before he finally fell asleep.

* * *

The next morning, Stig had a fever and could not get out of bed. Hiding his anxiety as best he could, Gom nursed him, night and day, through the deep cold, sponging him with melted snow when the pump was frozen, spooning him hot broth made from their winter supplies in the root cellar, and heating stones at the hearth to warm his bed. As soon as he could sit up again, Stig was at the walking stick, chipping and sanding until the animals fairly leapt from the wood grain. Gom picked it up, turning it this way and that, then tried it for size, walking over to the hearth and back. "That's a fine stick, Father. As good a piece as ever you've made."

"Aye," Stig agreed, eyeing it critically. "It'll serve you well enough when I'm gone."

Gom strode back to the bed, laid the stick down on the cover. "It's a mite too tall for me, Father," he said lightly, but inwardly he grieved to hear his father speaking thus.

At last, Stig could stand again, and with the aid of his new walking stick, shuffle over to his chair by the fire.

"There you see, Father. Another few days and that stick will hang on the wall," Gom said. "And very decorative it'll look, too."

"That'd be nice," Stig said. "Very nice, but I'm not so sure, son."

Gom felt a catch of alarm at something in his father's voice. "Courage," he said. "The worst is over. Spring is almost here and time to fix the cart for our first trip down to Clack."

But a few days later, in that space when winter dragged its heels and it seemed that spring would never come, Stig rose from his bed in the middle of the night, went to sit in his rocking chair facing Wife's empty one, and died.

When Gom awoke at dawn, he found Stig in his chair

by the dead fire, looking for all the world as though he'd fallen asleep. "Father? Father! What are you doing out in the cold! For shame, and you still with your bad cough and all!" He reached out, took Stig's shoulder. It was heavy, and different. "Father!" He knelt down and looked into his father's face, and knew that Stig was no longer there.

He laid his head on Stig's knees and wept. For all his father's old fears about Gom leaving him in the middle of the night, it was Stig who had stolen away from him in the end.

Gom buried Stig in the frozen ground with a great effort that took him all the next day and late into the chilly night. This he had to do alone. He had no choice, for neither Hilsa nor Stok could make it up the mountain through that deep snow.

When Gom was done, he raised a cairn of gray mountain stone over his father's grave, through which Wind could sing, when it would.

"*Ooo*, now what?" Hoot Owl called from his high branch.

"My father's dead," Gom answered him. "He lies beneath these stones."

"Oh. I'm sorry to hear that. He was a good man. I shall miss his song."

Gom blinked up at him through his tears. That was the first compliment he'd heard Hoot Owl pay anybody.

"But what about you, young man? You'll be off now, I suppose?"

Gom, surprised, shook his head. "Oh, no. I'm staying here. I'm woodcutter now. I promised my father, you see."

Owl hooted derisively.

"You what? Just look at yourself! Woodcutter, indeed!"

"What do you mean?" Gom demanded, but Owl, still hooting, flew away.

Gom felt a sudden desire to go up to Mandrik's grave, to tell him what had happened, to relieve his troubled mind. But Mandrik had said, and Gom remembered well, that one was as much a fool alone on a mountain as in a crowd. If that were so, it should be as easy to be wise in a wooden hut as by an icy grave.

Gom went back inside the hut, and sat facing Stig's empty chair. He twirled the rune between his fingers, but there was no help in that. Since that far night under the mountain it had lain silent, leaving Gom to make his own choices. "Father," he said. "I'm getting ideas about going away. Mandrik said that I have gold locked up inside me that I must take out into the wide world. He said also that I had to return Mother's rune to her. I couldn't tell you at the time, for it would only have made you disquiet. I believe him, Father. He knew her name. Harga. Harga the Brown. I could never tell you, without telling you the rest. But that's all right, for you always called her, Wife. So now I must decide. Should I keep my promise to you and stay, and be woodcutter as you want me to? Or take my chances out in the wide world, Far Away?"

He sat there, facing his father's chair, waiting for an answer.

Stay. The words came quite clearly into his mind. He must stay. A promise was a promise. His father had known that Gom would get into hot water the moment his back was turned. *You're . . . but a simple mountain boy and ignorant of the great wide world out there.* That was why he'd made Gom vow to stay safe on Windy Mountain, doing the one thing he was fitted for.

His mother's true son, Stig had also called him, often.

Had recognized the restless in him. Poor Father, to have worried so over his son all these years. Well, Gom would stay and try to live up to Stig's hopes and expectations even though his father might never know.

He dozed a little, woke with the word *gold* on his lips.

Skeller and his gold.

No. Not Skeller. Mandrik.

What had Mandrik said? Gom hadn't thought of it these many years.

That he who buried a thing of great price deserved to lose it. And that if Gom was his mother's true son, he must go and find her.

Your way lies over the mountains. . . .

But those were words only, from a man long dead.

He'd promised his father he'd stay.

He thought of the years ahead: of living up in the hut as his father had before him. Of chopping wood, and carting it down the mountainside to bargain with Bok, and Craw, and Pinkle, and company.

That was belonging.

He thought of Stok and his brood. Of Hilsa and Horvin and the rest. All in their warm cottages with their children, webbed in with mothers and fathers, sons and daughters, grandmas and grandads, and uncles and aunts.

He thought of himself. Up in the hut alone. Cutting wood. Taking it down. Pulling the empty cart back up. Cutting more wood. Taking it down. Round and round and round.

That was *belonging*?

What had he said to Wind once? "Whatever folk say of me in future, good or bad, I'll not heed, but just stay true to myself." Fine words, bravely spoken, lightly forgotten, and here he was, pledged to serve folk who at last might need him, but who would never like him or accept him. Not really, for all his efforts.

Gom sighed. What of his own pledge to himself? Wasn't that more important than his promise to his father, who, after all, wanted only his safety?

On a sudden thought, he reached into his right back pocket and took out a small leather pouch. Loosing the drawstring, he shook out his old treasures into his open palm: seeds, the pod of a hoarbell, a honeybee's sac, the cocoon of a moon moth, and—a tiny fleck that flashed in the glow of the firelight.

A gold flake, scored by a crude thumbnail, but still a gold flake.

He stared at it long, then, carefully restoring it to the pouch, he put the pouch back in his pocket and stood up.

He doused the fire, washed his dishes, folded up Stig's bedclothes, and swept the floor. Then he filled his pockets with the last of the bread and aged cheese.

Time to go.

He stood for a moment looking into the dark of the little room that smelled of woodsmoke and broth and Stig's poultices still. Then taking up his father's carved walking stick, he quietly closed the door behind him.

He trudged the few paces through the snow to the cairn. Like a staff, the stick was, rather than a walking stick, with the sparrow looking ahead to spy out the way. "Goodbye, Father. Sleep well." He bowed his head sadly before the cairn of stones, its chinks already filled with fine drifting snow. He stood for a moment, remembering Stig's voice ringing over the treetops. And as he stood, he became aware of a faint, melodious humming coming from the region of his chest. The rune!

He slipped his hand inside his jacket and pulled it out.

The fine curious markings were shining like fine gold thread, and sparks ran up and down the sides. From deep within it came the sound of bees humming in a midsummer glade, and Wind through the high pines. Gom stepped up to the cairn and, taking the rune from around his neck, slipped his hand through the stones over the dark space within.

There he stood, the tears flowing down his cheeks, holding the singing rune until the sound faded, until all that was left was the sound of the real wind keening through bare branches. He pulled back his hand. The rune was dark again, and silent. Sadly, Gom replaced it about his neck.

"Go," he urged himself, turning away. "Go now or you never will." He trudged across the clearing, but instead of turning left down the track he went on through the deep snow to the limestone caves.

CHAPTER TWENTY-SIX

OODBYE, SESSERY," he called through her front door. "I hope you hear me this time, for I'm going away. Thanks for all you've taught me. I shan't forget you."

MMMmmmnn, I know you won't, came the mocking reply. *You'll never escape me. I'm not like you, with your "me"s and "thee"s. Wherever you go there'll be a relative of mine and that will be me. So: fare-you-well! And watch your step.* Her laughter drifted through the caverns and away.

He crunched on through the snow to Mandrik's grave.

It looked bleak and ghostly in the moonlight, rigid in its cap of ice.

"Goodbye, Mandrik," he said. "I'm off, just as you said I would be." He waited, hoping as always, for a sign that Mandrik had heard him, but there was only the crystal sound of water over icicles and the swish of the stream brushing the frozen bank.

He went down to the trail in a wide arc, passing the old places where he'd played while Stig chopped his wood.

Hoot Owl flew by.

"What? Not gone yet?" he called. "I hoped you'd seen reason at last, young Gom."

"Aye," Gom said, and sighed heavily.

"So now then," the owl coughed and fluffed out his feathers. "Off with you before you change your mind. Don't worry, your father will never be lonely. And between Wind and me he'll never want for a song. And shouldn't, so many wonderful ones he's shared with us over the years. I'll sorely miss his voice." He looked down on Gom and solemnly winked an eye. "I confess I'll even miss you too, even though I will be able to snooze in peace from now on. Now: toodle-oo. I still have hunting to do!"

With an abrupt flick of his wings, Hoot Owl flew off into the dark.

Gom set off down the mountain, down the old trail made unfamiliar by deep snow. Now and again he stopped and looked back up, remembering the times he and his father had climbed it, the songs they'd sung, the yarns they'd spun.

And the friends he'd made and buried over the years.

The trail was heavy going. The snow was still deep in pockets; sometimes so hard that he had to slide perilously over ice, careening down the crazy zigzag path, bucking and flying head over heels over sudden roots and boulders, to land in holes where snow had drifted soft as down. But most of the time because of the dense trees and steep clefts he had to walk, and climb, and scramble down the ice-locked way. His legs began to ache, and his clothes clung where snow had stuck and melted on him.

Partway down, Wind changed about, kindly blowing on his back.

So! You thought to slip off without saying goodbye, eh!
Wind teased, gently ruffling Gom's hair.

"Never," Gom said. "I was hoping rather that you'd
go with me until I find my feet."

*That will I. In fact, like Sessery, I'll always be with
you, or some relative of mine will, which is the same thing.
Say when you're ready.*

"I'm that now," Gom said, "but I've just one last thing
left to do."

After you, Wind said, and helped Gom along the rest
of the way.

It was just dawn when he reached the town.

It looked closed and dormant, with great ridges piled
along the curbs, blocking off the sidewalks, putting the
houses under a sort of siege.

As he trudged along he couldn't help but notice the
woodpiles by the house walls on either side of him. Quite
low, they were. Gouged almost to the ground. Soon it would
be spring and time for the woodcutter to bring down the
year's first load to start building them up again. But that
woodcutter would not be Gom Gobblechuck.

Midway along the street, the great bell hung, stiff with
icicles. Gom paused for a moment. Only too soon, its sound
would fill the valley.

He went on sadly to Hilsa's cottage and rapped the
knocker three times.

"Why, Gom!" Hilsa's face was full of sleep, her hair,
tousled. "Is it—oh no!" She covered her face with her hands.

Gom put a hand on her shoulder, patted it awkwardly.
"There, there, Hilsa. Don't cry. You knew he wasn't well.
You told me yourself the last time we were down here—"

"I know, I know, but it's one thing to know it in your
head. It's quite another to—to—oh, Gom! I thought he'd
make it through the winter, at least!" She began to sob.

Gom walked her into the cottage and shut the door behind them. A voice called sleepily through the open bedroom door. "Hilsa? What is it?"

"Hilsa," Gom said. "Look, don't think ill of me. I've buried Father real fine, and left the cottage clean and nice. But I must go, and now before I change my mind."

Hilsa looked up, shocked. "*Go?* Go where?"

"Just between you and me, to look for Mother."

Hilsa stared at him blankly. "For Mother? Have you gone crazy?" Her tears forgotten, she took his shoulders now and sat him down. "This business with Father has stirred your mind. Now, you just bide here, while I make you—"

Gom stood up. "Nay, Hilsa. Don't make it any more difficult. I hope we meet again one day. And I wish you well. But for now I must be going."

He reached up and placed a quick kiss on her cheek, then made for the door. She was still calling him back as he closed the picket gate behind him and walked on up the street, his throat all lumpy and dry.

He struggled through to Stok's house, and knocked on his door.

"Why, Gom!" Stok cried. "Come in, come in!"

But this time Gom stayed out on the doorstep.

"Father's dead," he said. "His cairn's behind the hut. Clack must find itself a new woodcutter now. Horvin's a good strong lad." Great Horvin, who still loafed about doorways, unable, as he put it, to "find his proper 'nitch.' "

"Oh dear," Stok said. Then, "Hey!" he cried, as Gom's words dawned on him. "Whatever do you mean? Come inside and talk proper. If Father's dead, you must stay with Hilsa or me until the thaw when we can get back up with you to keep wake. Then we'll speak about your future. You're woodcutter now. You promised Father!"

"I did?" Gom's eyes gleamed. "And how would you know that?"

"Well, Gom." Stok's eyes shifted a bit. "Somebody had to—I mean— Father did tend to leave things—"

"You mean," Gom said, "that you put him up to it?"

"Don't take it like that, Gom. We had a talk last fall. You know I only meant well." Stok's children crowded the doorway behind their father, all eyes and ears.

"Shut that door, Stok!" Ditty shouted. Her voice over the years had sharpened to a nagging whine. "I'm a-trying to get this fire to light—that is if you want breakfast."

"Come in," Stok said again. "At least stay for a bite before you go. Just to show we've no hard feelings between us. Why, you're *smiling*! How can you, at a time like this?"

"Because," Gom said, embracing Stok warmly, "I felt so bad at breaking my word to Father. But now I see that I'm not at all!" He stepped down off the step, all serious again. "I'm glad you told me, Stok. For my own peace of mind. And I know you were only looking out for me, as you've always done. You've always been a good brother to me, the very best. I'll really miss you, Stok." His hand firmly about Stig's walking stick, Gom turned from him, then back again. "Goodbye. I hope we meet again some day." He swallowed hard. How could he turn his back on his brother's face, and he looking so upset and all.

From down the street there came the first tolling of the bell.

Gom went through the gate and shut it behind him. On either side of the snowy street, townsfolk were coming out to stare. In the distance Hilsa's figure, all bundled up, toiled through the snow toward him.

Gom began to walk rapidly away.

"But, where are you going?" Stok shouted over the gate.

"Far Away," Gom called over his shoulder.

"But why? *Why!*"

"Because my way lies over there," Gom answered, and with that, he walked steadfastly down to the end of the street, over the snow-covered no-man's-land, past Maister's cabbage patch and the rigid scarecrow with its frozen plume: through and out.

WINDY MOUNTAIN SONG

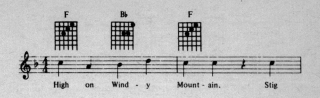

High on Wind-y Mount-ain. Stig

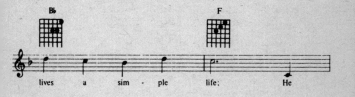

lives a sim-ple life; He

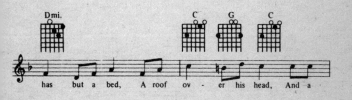

has but a bed, A roof ov-er his head, And a

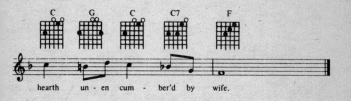

hearth un-en cum-ber'd by wife.

STIG'S SONG

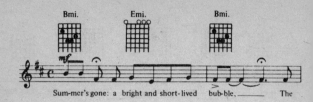

Sum-mer's gone: a bright and short-lived bub-ble, _____ The

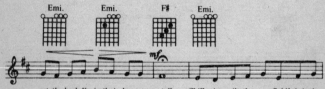

cat-tle hud-dle in their hay-warm stalls; Chill mists wilt the corn-field's brit-tle

stub-ble _____ And seas-on'd logs lie ti-dy by the walls.

Sheep crop close the au-tumn fal-low;_ Smoke coils up from ev-'ry home-ly

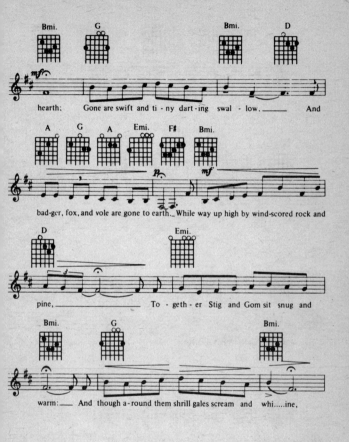

hearth; Gone are swift and ti - ny dart-ing swal - low.___ And

bad-ger, fox, and vole are gone to earth._ While way up high by wind-scored rock and

pine,_____ To - geth - er Stig and Gom sit snug and

warm:__ And though a - round them shrill gales scream and whi.....ine,

(Guitar 8va bassa)

There they'll stay con - tent and safe from harm.

THE FINCH AND SPARROW SONG

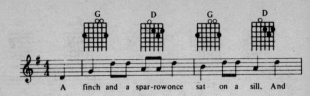

A finch and a spar-row once sat on a sill, And

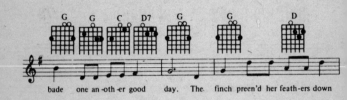

bade one an-oth-er good day. The finch preen'd her feath-ers down

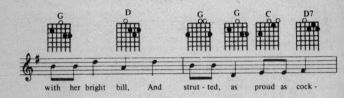

with her bright bill, And strut-ted, as proud as cock-

jay. "Brown spar-row," said finch, "pray, look your fill. Don't you

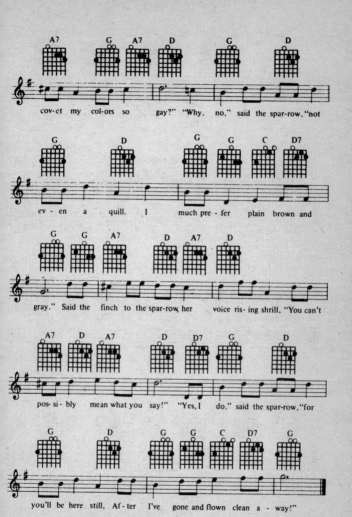

THE LOLLYBOB SONG

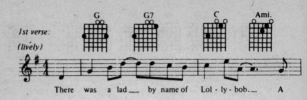

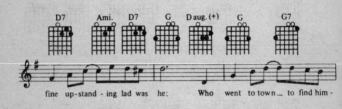

1st verse:
(lively)

There was a lad __ by name of Lol-ly-bob. __ A

fine up-stand-ing lad was he; Who went to town __ to find him-

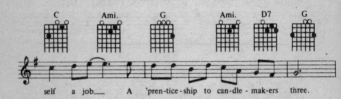

self a job. __ A 'pren-tice-ship to can-dle-mak-ers three.

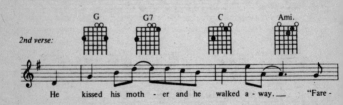

2nd verse:

He kissed his moth-er and he walked a-way. __ "Fare-

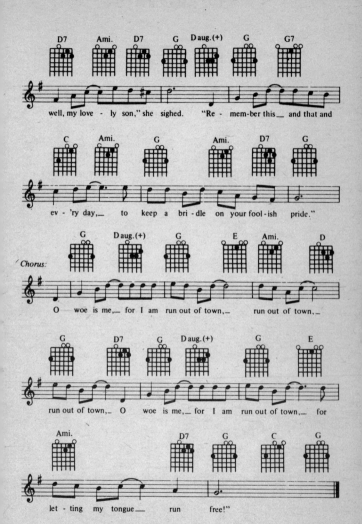